L U C I E ' S
L O N G   V O Y A G E

Lucie's Long Voyage is Alina Reyes' second novel.
Her first, *The Butcher*, was an international
bestseller and has been translated into fifteen
languages. Her new novel, *The Fatal Bodice* (*Au
Corset Qui Tue*), is currently available in hardback
from Methuen. Alina Reyes lives in Paris.

ALINA REYES

Lucie's Long Voyage

translated from the French by David Watson

Minerva

A Minerva Paperback
LUCIE'S LONG VOYAGE

First published in Great Britain 1992
by Methuen London
This Minerva edition published 1993
by Mandarin Paperbacks
an imprint of Reed Consumer Books Ltd
Michelin House, 81 Fulham Road, London SW3 6RB
and Auckland, Melbourne, Singapore and Toronto

First published as *Lucie au Long Cours* in 1990
by Editions du Seuil

Copyright © 1990 by Editions du Seuil
The author has asserted her moral rights
Translation copyright © 1992 by David Wright

A CIP catalogue record for this title
is available from the British Library

ISBN 0 7493 9966 X

Printed and bound in Great Britain
by Cox and Wyman Ltd, Reading, Berks

It is raining. I am writing.
The outside is my inside.

In this way the mountain gradually took its place inside me. Pushing like a fat stone it sometimes bumps up against my brow. In the coagulating ink, in the scratching of my pen, in the imprint of the letters on the page I want to see the stone flow out and take shape under my hand – now my familiar, my ally, no longer the invading stranger.

Sometimes the bear visits me in my dream. Like a vast, warm shroud his shadow bends over me, spreads out and embraces me. Passionately I grab hold of his fur, I open up to the violence of his scent, and I tremble with fear when his animal roar rises from the cavernous depths of his chest.
   Sometimes also I feel the beast living inside me; rolled into a ball, deep in my stomach, once it lay dozing. Now it is flexing itself in

my limbs, now the beast is impatiently making space for itself, straining my flimsy skin, stretching and spreading into my muscles in waves of heavy blood, attempting to open its muzzle in my jaws, flare its nostrils in my nose.

On certain nights when the moon is nearly full, at certain times when the tide sucks the sea far out into the distance, on certain futile days when empty gestures resound with the rumbling of the mountain, I unclench my mouth to the smell of my armpit, lying in the grass or spread against a tree, and I growl quietly, I growl as deep a growl as I can manage, under my breath, in the silence of the sky.

Starving, not knowing what it was I hungered for, just like billions of others the same, I lived out my hollow existence, dizzy and sorrowful like a question mark, its pot-bellied mass levitating absurdly above a minute planet of ink.

That day, my forehead pressed against the coach window, I watched the beautiful green meadows roll slowly by, the undulating expanse of soft grass and wild flowers, the whipped-cream clouds, lined with crevices of gold and caramel, and, rippling with a silky sheen between the arcs of the sky and the earth, the chocolate coats of the mares with their foals. Suddenly the mountain was there. The jagged line of the horizon, which seemed so far away, filled the space. The road began to climb and twist, the coach wheezed upwards. I felt I could almost touch the dark, bushy shape of the thickly-wooded foothills. I shuddered. Two bare, grey peaks had appeared, sharp and slightly tilted towards each other, touched, as if by the hand of God, by a shaft of sunlight bursting through a hole in the clouds.

The sun was setting. Dark forms flitted through the woods. The village came in sight. A tight huddle of grey houses with steep roofs and narrow windows. The coach drove past stone walls and parked in the narrow square in the shadow of the clock tower.

How was it that, as the road continued, as the mass of the mountains took over the terrain and imposed itself on me, the landscape I had found so pretty, so pleasant, so picture post-card, suddenly transformed itself into a dark heavy stone inside my chest?

My friend's house was at the end of a very

3

steep, narrow road more than twenty minutes' drive from the village. By the time I arrived the great slanting shadows had almost covered the rooftops. Tanned, dressed in shorts and a blouse, her hair bleached by the sun, Paula led me to her heavy old car and put my bag on the back seat. Soon the light went entirely, swallowed in the mist. From all sides a mass of cotton wool smothered up to the car windows. The car struggled round the hairpin bends, its yellow headlights piercing a wall of fog so thick it even deadened the sound of the engine. I could already feel the events of my normal life falling away in this slow, silent, opaque world on the edge of the ravine.

In daylight Paula's small grey house lies in a pretty green jewel-case, like a cairn marking the path across the grassy space, surrounded by high bare walls: to the right the great crags of Langheur, steep and towering, nesting-ground of vultures; and to the left the chiselled line of peaks that mark the frontier between the two countries, drawn five centuries ago when both sides judged this ridge to be the most difficult to cross in the whole range. On the same side, almost opposite the doorway of the house, and tilting towards each other in a strange, striking attitude, are the twin peaks of the dead Moon and the red She-wolf. From here, especially in the soft light of the setting sun, they look like two huge, swelling breasts, the nipples erect and both oddly straining towards the same point – squinting breasts.

From the valley their profile is entirely different: stuck there above the dark brow of the forest they look like the horns of some gigantic bull. Male? Female? The peaks of the Moon and the She-wolf make a strange couple.

The first morning, when I opened my shutters, when I saw the mountain there, framed in my small window, looking so monumental, I stuck out my head, and my shoulders, and finally my whole body in the desire to embrace it. I wanted to hold it against me and take it into me, I wanted to climb it, to follow the paths I could make out on its sides, to stumble against its mineral coarseness, its rough and secret faces . . . That night I had dreamed that a great big stone had fallen out of my mouth, and that I then had to open up my chest because I had a tooth sticking in my heart, deep inside me, under my left breast.

*

In the haze of dawn the mountain was cold and distant. Bathed in mystery, the peaks rose into a sky the colour of stone. I took the rocky path, and went into the forest.

Beneath the trees the air was cool and damp. Above me and below me a host of long, thin, tightly packed trunks grew vertically from the slope, forming acute angles with it. There were dark rocks cluttered around, speckled with moss. I stopped walking for a few moments to look at the misty, motionless, precipitous mass of firs and beeches, frozen in a silence only accentuated by the occasional echo of a cracking twig, a heavy beating of wings, a fretful cry.

The soil, still wet from the morning dew, caked my shoes, and my legs felt heavier with every step as I stuck in the mud. The surface of the path was loamy and scored by gulleys. I looked for a stick to help me on my way. Spiders' webs, glistening with pearls of dew, hung their weary light between the branches. Next to a bilberry bush I picked up a piece of wood which I could use as a walking stick. I was tempted to taste the berries, but the cold, and perhaps also their colour, made me shiver, and I gave them a miss.

Finding a stick was a good move. The path

soon became very steep and seemed even more muddy. I scrutinised it closely, trying to locate the least difficult route, and generally I avoided the middle in favour of one side or the other where there were rocks or low branches to hold on to. The thick layer of clay stuck to the soles of my shoes made them particularly slippy, and I skidded a few times, though without falling over. I had mud stains right up my legs as far as the hem of my shorts.

Thanks to my exertions a warmth had spread through my body, and with it a feeling of jubilation. The earth smelled sweet. 'I'm shaping it with my steps,' I said to myself; it felt like a fiancée, whose arm I would have squeezed a thousand times, a tender, restive fiancée I refrained from laying myself upon forever.

Here and there among the rocks sprouted large flowers with purple clusters, or with yellow corollas opening on a black pistil, sticking out like a tongue. I looked at them, breathed them in, ran my finger gently up the stem and over the fine petals, trying to read each flower like a word from the earth.

A black moss crept up the sides of the huge trees, almost monstrous with its long living filaments cast wide like antennae, where glimmers of light, filtered through the vault of leaves, hung in green flashes. On some trunks families of white mushrooms without stalks were ranged in steps like staircases climbing to the chiaroscuro of the foliage. Orange-striped salamanders scuttled over the carpet of dead leaves where thick black slugs slithered.

In the shade of the undergrowth the ground was deep in humus and plants with pungent scents, sometimes sickly sometimes musky, scents of skin and armpits, scents of warm flesh still soft from a long bath. I thought I could sense walking by my side a little woman with an ape's head, that Lucy who died at the age of twenty more than three million years ago, and whose bones had been preserved in the ground. When she was exhumed, Lucy, the primitive, remained impregnated with the perfume of the earth, just as the earth remained impregnated with that of her flesh, and in the strange silence of the trees I followed this mixture of perfume, that of the distant Ethiopian, my human and animal sister, and that of the soil, bed of the dead and the alluvium of life, moulded by an ancient god to form the first being.

So I continued, guided by this sickly companion with her coarse features. And little by little, by outwitting the mud, by learning to spot the best route, the best place to put my feet and the best form of foothold, the best grip on the smooth rocks, the best posture to maintain balance, I felt myself become as elastic as the mud, which now covered my hands and legs. I was a woman of mud, of earth and of sky, a malleable body through which the forest breathed, steamy with a mixture of water and air; with the trees and the sodden path I was the soft breath and tongue of the great body of the mountain stretching its concrete mass towards the world. I threw my stick away when I saw the gap of light at the end of the path.

The sun was already high, and the mountain before me was covered with white stones. I sat down under the last tree in the forest, a large fir. In its shadow the rocks were softened in patches by a rich, fresh moss. A sweetish odour of sweat rose from my body.

My shoes were heavy with the mud, a thick layer which formed a second sole. I started to clean them. The earth was still gluey, like over-damp bread dough. I wondered what it tasted like. I licked my hand to try to wash the stains off my thighs, but only succeeded in making my palms sticky.

I now had to face the stones, baked white by the midday sun, the piles of rubble which pitted the path wedged into the slope of shale, running uphill like a goat.

Night was falling. I had lost my way and had no hope of finding it again before morning. Four vultures circled slowly. The mountain seemed infested with these menacing creatures. At first I admired their wingspan, their amazing skill in riding thermals in the air. But it is because of them that I got lost.

After leaving the forest I had followed the path which tacked between the Moon and the She-wolf. In the afternoon the sound of sharp cries made me look up. Emerging from behind the Moon a dozen tawny vultures, followed by a flock of alpine choughs, began circling above my head. Their dark shapes stood out sharply against the blue sky. Dazzled, I suddenly left the path and started climbing along the slope of the She-wolf, running and stumbling over its black stones, trying to get closer to the birds, which I never let out of my sight. I stopped only to contemplate their immense wings which tapered into feathers like fingers. I was fascinated by their mastery of the air. They circled eternally, as if enacting some ritual. I imagined their small heads with their sorcerers' masks. I managed to get quite close to them, and their cries pierced my eardrums. I quivered with joy.

However, they were circling further away, and I had to keep running so as not to lose them from view. Finally they peeled off one by one. The sky emptied, the silence returned, and I found myself alone, perched on the side of the She-wolf, far from the path which I could make out down below me. The sun was beating down directly, it was scorching hot. The blood was pounding in my temples, sweat trickled down my neck, my throat was burning.

I wanted to rejoin the path, but the slope was much too steep, and also slippery. It was a gigantic, chaotic scree-slope of jagged marl, an arid black wound attesting to some ancient convulsion of the mountain. I fell down; the second time, reaching out ahead to steady myself, I plunged my hand into a thistle. I chose the least difficult slope; by going round the left side of the She-wolf I hoped to rejoin the path further on, and then retrace my route back to the house. Every now and again I stopped to squeeze my palm between my nails to pull out some tiny thorn.

In concentrating on each spot where I put my feet I had wandered away from the She-wolf and, with night falling, I had not yet rediscovered my path.

I came onto some flat terrain, crossed by a stream and strewn with large boulders, surrounded by mountains which seemed far away and which were streaked in shadow. I spotted an elongated white boulder which widened near the top on one side, forming a sort of canopy. I decided to use it as a shelter for the night. I thought it was only a short walk away, but I noticed that it came no nearer as I advanced towards it. As the shadows and the light evolved, its colour seemed to change from white to red, then a mixture of grey and black, but in such a way that its contours seemed to change several times, and in the end I wondered if I was still looking at the same rock.

However, I finally got close enough to touch it, and I discovered that it was nothing like how I had seen it from a distance, when I thought it was quite near. It was a large round grey rock, offering only a tiny space by way of shelter, which I would have had difficulty squeezing into. I sat down with my back against the rock.

I regretted having come so far from the stream without realising. Down below I spotted one or two flashes of light which signalled its presence; I could still hear the faint sound of it babbling over the rocks. It was now very cold, and I couldn't think of anything else to do except curl up in a shivering ball to try to conserve a little heat. I noticed that I had passed to another side of the She-wolf and the Moon, which now stood one slightly behind the other, their horned silhouette illuminated by a golden ray cast by the full moon – a huge, tawny moon enthroned right between the two peaks.

After lying ages prostrate in the cold I finally fell into a sleep troubled by dreams. The world had foundered in a nuclear disaster, and in order to avoid decomposition I immersed my face in a large pool of quicklime. The lime was soft and oily like a cream, and when I plunged my face right into it I felt no burning nor any need to breathe, but rather a sort of pleasure. Then I returned to the ruined world, now protected, but with my skin all burnt behind my white mask.

I woke up at the end of my dream. The moon had become a whitish colour, like an over-ripe cheese, and its creamy light flowed over me. I was overcome with dizziness and almost passed out in the shadow of the rock, my hands clenched over my tight chest. Then I went back to sleep and had exactly the same dream.

A huge growl woke me with a start. I was completely numb with the cold and at first I felt I couldn't move. I opened my eyes. I was lying in cloud, it was daybreak. I turned round and I saw towering in front of me in the mist the colossal mass of a dark brown bear standing on his hind legs.

The bear growled again as he looked sideways at me, seemed to search for something at his feet, then dropped onto his side and lay there motionless, his head resting on his paws, his gaze fixed and distant, with eyelids half-closed. I thought my chest had exploded, and the mountain had rocked. The bear could just as easily have lain down on me and crushed me into the rock with his entire weight. But he remained strangely impassive as if, having

14

overcome his surprise and perhaps his fright, he had recognised me as an inoffensive creature, one he perhaps felt drawn to in some way.

The bear yawned, and I saw his tongue was blue. I managed to breathe out. A light breeze shifted the cloud, which broke up at ground level, and the sky began to appear. With tears and laments, which came out of my mouth looking like smiles, I began to speak.

'We are a people in distress,' I said. And I cried a bit more.

The bear stirred his enormous bulk, sat on his hind paws, pressed his muzzle towards me as I carried on talking. He gazed into my face sedately. I felt the blood flow to my cheeks. I almost reached out my arm towards him, as if to shake his hand. But the wind reminded me of his wild animal smell and I withdrew my gesture.

The bear rocked his head, in an ample gesture which I often saw him repeat later, stretched out his neck, nostrils flared, then with a movement of extraordinary suppleness did an about-turn. I thought I could see a ribbon running the length of his heavy body, down the line of his fur, twisting and unrolling as rapidly as a banner in the wind. He moved off swiftly on all fours.

I was astonished. The rock was cold and hard under my knees. I was alone. 'Bear!' I cried. But he carried on his way as if he had heard nothing, as if mocking mankind, and particularly this delirious woman lost in the mountains. I started to run after him, after his brown bulk which threaded its way among the rocks. My breath dug holes in me, to the pit of my stomach, my mouth was enlarged, frozen in a rictus. My feet struck the ground, one after the other, my heart galloped, everything jumped, the rocks, the stones, the sky and the animal, up ahead, still out of reach.

Then as I almost caught up with him the bear disappeared into the ravine. From the edge of the path I saw him calmly loping down the sheer slope.

In front of me lay a rocky abyss, its steep side was strewn with thin trees and bushes the colour of verdigris, and at its base I could hear the roar of a torrent. A bare sheer wall formed the opposite slope of the gorge. I sat down, and with the help of my feet and hands, the ridges and vegetation, I began to slide down the slope on a traverse. I had lost sight of the bear, and my only thought was to catch up with him. No danger could have prevented me from following my course, from obeying the imperious force which drove me.

Before long I had to turn to face the rock to continue my descent. I groped my way down, hanging by my hands and peering around below to seek out new footholds. My hands were burning, the rocks and branches left bruises on my face, my stomach, my knees, the inside of my arms. He had looked at me, I wasn't through with him yet. This violent hand-to-hand with the mountain was my declaration.

The rock was now greenish-blue and damp, and bristling with cracks like a gigantic block of quartz; the covering of vegetation sprouted ever thicker, exuberant masses of flowers whose colours, alternatively dark, soft, golden, deep, cast waves of green light. I slithered more than climbed down the clammy pillars through the ferns whose scent made me feel dizzy.

The only way to reach the bottom was to follow every accident of the terrain, to know it through the gropings of my body, to make it my ally through close and constant contact. It felt like my blood was running for joy beneath my skin. Each breath I drew breached my nostrils and lips, carried me further down, promised me my goal, in a movement of infinite slowness where time seemed annihilated, arrested all around me as I descended, hugging matter, descended.

Gradually the sound of a waterfall filled the air. Fearing that an attack of vertigo might cause me to fall into the gap, I tried not to look either up or down. I simply held tighter against the oozing rock which I pressed with my cheek or licked occasionally. I arrived in a shadowy region, crossed by trickles of water. I let myself slide down a gently inclined plane to an opening in the rock from which the waterfall emerged.

The water came out of the mountain through a sort of basin and fell like a smooth turquoise scarf to the nearby base of the ravine, where it joined the course of a fairly broad transparent stream. My throat was dry, and urged on by the sight of the water which I had not been able to reach in the hollow of the rock I finished my descent as quickly as I could.

I drank from my cupped hands, I bathed beneath the waterfall. Raising my head I saw, further along, amazingly high up, the lips of the gap, hemmed with bushes, and, flowing through it, a deep shaft of daylight falling as far as the pebbles which glistened beneath the water.

Following the stream, I entered the gorge. The gap narrowed increasingly, to the extent that I was soon having to clamber over large boulders which blocked my way. The water had disappeared beneath the piles of stones. The light scarcely penetrated as far as the floor of the gorge. I arrived in a place of shadow, silence and cold. My blouse was still soaked from the waterfall, the icy fabric stuck to my back.

I was exhausted, and the going was still hard. I forced myself to go on a little further. I wouldn't have had the strength to climb back the way I came down. I needed to find a spot where the gorge opened out, where the slope was gentler and presented fewer problems. Before turning back to explore the side I had forsaken, to the right of the waterfall, I wanted to be sure that there was no possible way out down here.

I soon discovered among the scree what appeared to be the entrance to a cave. The opening was less than a metre across, and indeed seemed to get narrower inside, but I got a whiff of hope when I noticed a bright patch of light at the other end.

My knees trembled with each step, I shivered, the shadow thickened more and more. I didn't hesitate long. I pushed my upper body into the hole, then, crawling on my belly, my arm ahead of me, my eyes fixed on the bright spot, I began to move through the narrow passage. In some places I was held completely fast in the tube of rock, enclosed by the cold hard shaft, and I had to wriggle my shoulders, my spine and my hips to work myself loose, to free my bones from the stone's embrace.

Finally, I arrived in a sort of soft niche, a room vaulted like a four-poster bed, where the air was warm. The ray of light splayed out from a small, window-like hole in the dark wall to the right.

The bed was warm and soft and l curled up even more in the hollow of his fur. There was something big breathing next to me, I gripped it in my fists. I saw the light through my eyelids, but I didn't open my eyes, and with a sigh of well-being I went back to sleep.

*

When I woke up it took me a few moments to recognise the little cave and piece together the adventure which had led me here. What madness made me set off on this incredible chase, and how had I managed the difficult descent to the bottom of the ravine? If it hadn't been for the painful reminders of my escapade all over my body I would have doubted my memory.

I must have collapsed with fatigue on reaching the cave and fallen asleep. How could I have slept so soundly during such a long night lying on the hard rock?

I felt hunger gnawing in my stomach. I had to get out of this place as quickly as possible. At least that's how I rationalised it, mechanically, since oddly enough I didn't feel worried. I even smiled at the ray of light cutting cleanly through the air, free of floating dust.

I was covered with cuts and bruises, every muscle in my body was stiff. Limping, moaning, jeering myself on, I dragged myself to the opening. I had sprained a toe tripping over the heaps of stones piled up near the cave; it was now swollen and blue and I couldn't place it on the ground.

At first I had to close my eyes, so strong was the light and so sharp the contrast with the dark corner of the cave where I had slept. When I opened them I discovered a vast blue expanse glittering in the sun. It was a large lake, surrounded by a circle of imposing mountains, among which I recognised the Moon and the She-wolf, even though their profile looked different from here. I was confused as to my exact position.

Kneeling down, with my hands gripping the edge of the hole on each side of my chin, I admired the landscape. There was no path to be seen. It was as if no man had ever cast eyes on this magnificent scene. The sky had the colour of the lake, only transparent, shaded off, as if it had taken it after a long journey from the dark irradiating depths of the water. The highest peaks were crowned with snow, white streaks of névé lay on their flanks.

Suddenly the bear appeared. I was astonished. He was beautiful, simply beautiful, supple and serene in the heart of this wild nature. He walked softly and his hump quivered on his back as waves of light flowed across his dark fur. He stopped and turned his head towards me. His neck stretched out, his mouth open, he sniffed the wind. I quickly hid behind the rock. I heard him growl.

The silence returned. I risked another look through the opening and I saw him frolicking in the lake, then swimming across and popping up on another bank, his pelt soaked and dripping, and slipping off between two hills where I lost sight of him.

I was hungry and thirsty. I waited, surveying every nook and cranny. When I was more or less certain that he had gone, I pulled myself up and out of the cave.

I felt a fresh breeze. Standing upright I admired the breathtaking splendour of the scene. I thought I heard the sound of huge gongs, and I felt like crying.

I walked towards the lake, painfully. Because of my injured toe I was dragging my left leg and stepping only on the heel. The water in the lake was icy. I crouched down and drank it in handfuls, then lapped it up straight from the lake, my mouth placed on the limpid surface.

Later, with my heel burning with pain, I abandoned my upright posture and crawled around on all fours among the bushes bearing the red fruit, and emerged sated, my lips and cheeks tarred with sugary wine-coloured juice.

*

I spent the rest of the day in the cave, dozing and dreaming about the silence of the mountain, a silence which penetrated these walls muffled, sonorous and full like the voice of a bow sliding very slowly along the bass strings of a cello.

Now and again I dragged myself over to the opening and looked at the mountains, the sky and the water. In the middle of the afternoon I went out again to drink from the lake and to suck a few herbs and bilberries. In the evening the bear returned. I saw him in the shadows, treading nonchalantly through the rocks. I felt very weary. I returned to my bed and went straight to sleep.

I had three more warm gentle nights, wrapped as in an intimate penetrating dream in a mass of muscles and hairs. I would wake at dawn, alone and at peace. With a smile I would say: 'Bear'; then I would go out to quench my thirst in the lake. When the bear appeared I no longer hid, but I observed him from afar, impassioned. Occasionally he would growl in my direction, as if to keep me at a distance. Heavy and agile, sombre and light, he was the most beautiful wild animal, the most obvious presence in the world.

By the morning of the fourth day I was healed and able to walk again on both feet.

At dawn on the fourth day I left the cave. The mountains disappeared into a thick grey mist. The lake, its surface invisible, seemed transformed into a huge pit exhaling rose-coloured vapours, ghostly fumes, which alone defined its contours. I advanced cautiously through the rocks into the fog. As I approached the shore I heard noisy breathing, something splashing in the water.

I went into the water. The cold bit into my ankles, then rose through my body as I walked towards the noise. I heard crows cawing. The water gripped my chest like pincers. My limbs were tetanised, I was on the brink of sinking into the icy pit, when I reached out my hand to the dark mass which emerged from the mist. I heard a long soft growl, I felt myself taken and held against a warm body which danced me round in the water in waltz time.

The bear put me down between the walls of stone, in the spot where a ray of warm sunlight fell. Down on all fours he shook himself dry. Large drops of water splashed from his pelt, and I drew my arm across my cheek; more water dripped heavily from his belly. With his awkward precise walk he approached my curled up body, and lowered his large head towards me. A strong smell rose from his damp fur; I felt his warm steady breath. He sniffed my neck, and began licking my legs.

How could we live in such proximity, even as a bear and a woman, without forming more intimate ties? When each night I prayed for the bear to return, when at dawn, in the dark of the cave, I embraced him, when I kissed his claws, when I lay in his warmth, was I not simply being human?

We normally think we need to be loved. But we have more need to love, to dissolve ourselves, forget ourselves in the other. The other must be dangerous, enough to fear that he might refuse you, or absorb you totally – that, in one way or another, he might negate you. That he might force you to lose yourself or recognise yourself through this negation, destroy yourself or reconstruct yourself on the basis of it.

I have kissed the bear's clawed paws, I have known that fervour, that delicious annihilation of offering myself up totally, I have often crawled at the feet of the bear in the cave, I have wanted him to take me to the point of making me disappear. Who better than a wild animal to threaten actually to devour you, to stop the passage of time for you, to reserve for you, wolf-like, a place in the closed space of his belly, close by your ancestors, a place where the separation of beings and ages is abolished, where the dreams of men, of beasts, of trees and of each element join together in a single dream.

The bear had for me the extremes of wildness and delicacy. When I provoked him, curling up my lips, letting out piercing cries from the depths of my stomach, he would rise up before me, nostrils quivering, breathing powerfully, snarling in a low growl. He and I, two animals, we would confront each other, half-serious, half-playful, roll around together, biting each other's mouths, punching and clawing. Even though the bear measured his strokes so as not to injure me I expected at any moment to see his green eyes flashing in the shadows, to feel his jaws close furiously around my neck.

Like the bear I fed mainly on berries. I gorged myself with bilberries and cranberries, tasted the last of the strawberries, gathered raspberries, discovered edible mushrooms, roots and herbs. With great care I introduced my palate to new tastes, learnt to appreciate them. I captured insects, ants, crickets, cockchafers, crunched them between my teeth. I dismembered them, peeled the ones which were protected by hard shells – glistening golden or flesh-coloured beetles – savoured their flesh, as fine as the filling of delicate soft-centred sweets. I was still a woman, I still marvelled at the beauty of the mountain and made up songs while bathing in the lake.

One morning, at dawn, I had an attack of nausea. I remembered that I had not had a period for a long time. I was expecting a baby.

Standing against a tree the bear would claw deep into the bark. Or he would scratch his back against it with growls of pleasure, shedding several tufts of down, long brown shiny hairs. I would watch him, then I would go and rub myself against his spine, slowly, from my shoulder to my ankles. I would flex my own muscles against the powerful musculature of the animal, curry myself against his fur. Tender as a soft toy, the bear would embrace me with his heavy diligent paw, place his quivering muzzle on my neck, and stay like that, motion-less, attentive and docile.

With his massive paws the bear was the most skilful in the world at raking bilberry bushes, turning over large rocks, collecting ants.

One night, I ventured out in his tracks and found him, in the blueish light of a thin cres-cent moon, devouring the remains of some stinking carrion.

I never tired of admiring my lover's beauty, his strength, his suppleness, his perfect skill for living. And as I now went round naked, I also saw at each moment my own beauty, the glow-ing body of a woman who is loved.

Every morning, in the back of the cave, I slept in the bear's warmth, rolled up in the might of his limbs, disappearing and then being reborn in his embrace.

In the afternoons I wandered round the lake, and became familiar with every inch of my domain. It was warm, and the water took on the colour of emeralds in the light. On the shore a few large stones, bunches of resplendent

multicoloured flowers and fragrant herbs
marked out the gardens where I would stretch
out, recite words at random, doze off. Elsewhere, grey rocks sheltered the nests of rep-
tiles. Motionless lizards sunned themselves on
warm stones, their throats palpitating gently. I
would go close, look at the snakes with yellow
scales which would wind themselves around
each other, sometimes taking fright and flowing off smoothly into the shadows.

On moonlit nights I began following the bear
into the mountains. The bear covered a lot of
distance and I often lost sight of him in the
black and white flashes of rock and undergrowth. Then I would retrace my path and wait
a long time at the entrance to the cave, watching the moon or its reflection in the lake.

And gradually I came to adore the moon, or
rather to identify with it. That white star which
watched me in my solitude seemed to me like
the reflection of my belly, as if each called to
and attracted the other across the space
between sky and earth. When I watched it I had
peculiar desires, I formed habits related to its
nocturnal presence.

Squatting on a rock by the side of the lake I

would wait motionless, my hand dangling in the light-spangled water, until shoals of tiny silver fish emerged from beneath the stone. When I managed to catch one I would raise it up to the moon, my arm outstretched, then tear off its head and swallow the still wriggling body.

Or else, lying on my back, I would part my legs beneath the moon, my head upside down in the stars, and, softly at first, then ever more loudly, I would emit long hooting noises. Three nights in a row I climbed on the bear's back, thinking to get nearer to the creamy star, sticking out my tongue towards it as if to lick it, opening my mouth towards it as if to swallow it. But that did not satisfy my nameless desire: I formed a taste for sitting astride an oblong rock, which jutted out above the wide round pool of the lake, and biting it until my gums bled, with the growls and movements of a wild beast. Finally I would sleep from exhaustion, my legs and arms clasped tightly to the rock. At dawn I would drink the dew which had gathered in a hollow in the rock, before returning to the cave where the bear awaited me.

In the afternoon, when the weather is fine, I breastfeed Johnny at the Captain's grave. I sit on the rough grey stone, just next to the spot where the large crack slants across it. Some particles of earth must have found their way into the crack, for there are thin patches of moss and a few weeds growing in it.

The Captain's grave is in a quiet corner, at the end of the last alley on the left, in the oldest part of the cemetery. The sun's warmth is softened by the flickering shadows cast by the leaves of a tree I don't know the name of. No one comes, it is completely quiet, there are wild flowers at the foot of the enclosing wall. Baby John and I are totally at ease.

I have grown attached to this ship's captain, who ran aground here forty years ago. My visits to his grave are like a rendezvous. There are never any flowers there, it is obvious the world has long forgotten him. I talk to him, just in my head. If the dead can hear you then they can hear you just as well in your head as if you

33

talk out loud. I think the Captain is pleased by our visits. I lift my tee-shirt over my chest. Johnny sucks like a little darling. I'm sure we are pleasant company for a dead man.

My work requires me to visit all the cemeteries in town. But this one is my favourite. Very big, very old, near where I live, and I have a friend here. It is my garden, and the Captain's grave is my seat, my table, my bed. It is a playground for baby John. We sit there, the pair of us, without a sound, and time passes quietly. If you are really silent, silent even inside your head, you can hear the song of the dead. It is like a distant lullaby, a white lullaby without melody emerging from the mouths of statues or the moon, or even the hard bare bones sparkling in the earth.

A cemetery is a world unto itself. It is as though the air you breathe here is not quite the same as elsewhere. It quivers a little, perhaps. As if thousands of invisible people were breathing in secret. You know the dead no longer exist, but you also know that they are pleased when you are nice enough to come to see them. Because the first dead person you see is the one who is within us, of course. He is happy to see that you are thinking of him, that you care for him and have the goodness to make him feel at ease about his real birth to come, laid down in the warmth of the earth, in that soft silence so much appreciated by a few romantic young people, some mothers with their babies, some exhibitionists, some medical students with desecration in mind ... And you say to your dead person: 'That's life ...'

I don't like modern graves, all polished granite and harder than iron, spotless and gleaming like a fitted kitchen. I need stone which has lived, a bit blackened by pollution if necessary, with a rough surface which gets slightly warmer in the sun, graves which are no longer well tended, the earth long since undisturbed, where you can be sure that the dead person is finally free of the tears of family and friends, the pangs and complications of life, that he is now thinking only of his nuptials with the earth, of maturing like wine in a cask, of slipping out through the gaps in the wood of his coffin, of transforming his blood into sap, his flesh into humus, his bones into stone, his soul into leaves and flowers which will rustle up above, tickling the sky.

When it gets cooler we notice time has passed and we leave. Sometimes Johnny wants feeding again, so I offer him my breast, holding him tight so that he doesn't get cold. Then we return to the Belltower. As I carry him along he raises his head and opens his round eyes to look about. Johnny loves being on the move. Me too, and I often extend the journey to have more time to spend looking at people running in the streets, windows filing past, cars passing, stopping, starting off again, to see and hear the great merry-go-round of the town.

I go into the supermarket and buy bread, eggs or cheese, depending on what day it is, some fruit. When I'm flush I treat myself to a couple of cakes, a bar of good chocolate, sometimes even a roast chicken. I always go into the same shop, they know me, they don't keep an eye on me. That helps, because I often have to steal nappies for Johnny. I can't afford them. They'd probably be even less suspicious if I carried him in my arms, but I never take Johnny along if I have to steal something (nappies, I only steal nappies). I don't want him to know that his mother sometimes turns into a thief.

When I have to go to get some nappies, every week just about, I leave baby John all alone in the Belltower. All the time I'm out my mind is blank, consumed by terrible fears. What if baby

John managed to climb out of bed and crawl to the staircase, what if he fell, fell down the stairs to the floor of the church? . . . What if I were caught, what if I were arrested, and baby John were left all alone for the whole time? . . . What if I had to ask them to release me because my baby was waiting for me all alone in the Belltower? . . . What if they decided my baby couldn't stay with me, what if they took him away? . . .

Each time it is an exhausting ordeal, but I go on doing what I have to do, that is, making sure Johnny doesn't see me stealing and yet getting him nappies so that he is always clean, as I am myself. Down from where I live there is a tap for public use. Every day I carry up a large water bottle which I use for drinking, cleaning the dishes, washing my face and hands. For bathing and laundry I have a large vat which I keep down in the church. St Mark's has been unused for a long time, no one comes in. I can go around naked without fear. Often Johnny and I take the bus to the swimming baths, and spend hours of fun under the hot showers. My friends laugh at me because they have running water on every floor of the block where they are squatting, below the Granary. But I'm much better off in the Belltower, and even if they are my only friends I'll never go back to live with them.

In the beginning I had no particular plan to live in a church. I came to the Granary when I was pregnant, and it was something of a relief to have a roof over my head and some friends. But I soon got worried about the baby in my belly because of the fumes which always filled the room. And I didn't want to beg or deal in drugs in the metro like they do every so often. It was while walking one day in a cemetery that I had the idea of collecting pearls from abandoned wreaths to make into jewelry. It is delicate work and I enjoy it very much. I have always liked doing things with my hands. I sort out the pearls by size and colour, I design bracelets, brooches and necklaces in my mind, then I make them. With the very small pearls I weave motifs. Then I take my jewels to Rémi, who works in a large hairdresser's on the boulevards. He sells two or three a week, which gives me enough to buy food and some thread and clasps so I can carry on working.

As I spent my days walking in town to get some fresher air away from the Granary I often went into churches to have a rest – more often as my stomach expanded.

I prefer romanesque churches, all round and stony like bears' caves. Gothic churches are so elaborate that you almost forget they are made of stone. Churches are magic theatres, full of stories, pleasures and promises. In the first place there are the notices pinned to the porch: Mass times, works of charity, etc. You can imagine the lives of those sanctimonious old women, petit-bourgeois families and working people, for whom all this is important. Then you have to push open the wooden door, enter softly, without making a sound. If you were with someone you would be whispering; since you are alone you concentrate on not clicking your heels on the stone. The dark walls, the windows, the candles: you have entered a world of light and shadow, you feel quite small between these two great forces. Then there are statues, pictures, the altar, the gilding, the purple, all the propriety of Catholicism . . . All meant to impress you while signifying that it has all the importance of a game. You walk round with a measured step, your eyes raised to heaven, with the air of a respectful tourist. From the corner of your eye you see the young woman kneeling, her hands joined and her head bowed, all alone in her bubble. You want to burn a candle.

Then you sit down in the silence, and it is a bit like the cemetery, except that you are drawn upwards, rather than listening to the depths, except that the light is filtered and the wood of the seats is soft and polished, unlike the stone of the graves.

At first I didn't dare sit down. I had never learned how to use a church. I was afraid of not knowing, I was afraid above all of my emotions. Like the first time I kissed a boy. But then I got used to it, and all at once I understood that God is like lots of things, like love, like the dead or certain illnesses for example: he exists if you believe in him. And I felt I had the right to believe sometimes, and not believe most of the time. No one was asking me for a definitive yes or no. Do you need to make a definitive pronouncement on the reality of reflections? Reflections and shadows exist where there is a reflecting surface and a strong enough light to create them. Because they change and are not always there they prove that everything moves, that nothing is certain in this world, and that it would be most foolish to pretend otherwise.

Thus churches have become less authoritarian to me, and I have started frequenting them without any qualms.

It took me a long time to get used to my baby. In a way I didn't really know what a baby was until I had one. I only knew him as something inside me when he moved in my belly and gave me a kick. And then, all of a sudden, there he was with a human face. I remember how they placed him next to me in a transparent cradle at the maternity hospital. I looked at him, I was astonished. What I couldn't grasp was the fact that before there was nothing and now there was this ball of flesh, this being. Isn't it strange? We appear suddenly ... It is as if we make a hole in the void, a hole of living matter, in order to take our place in the world. And we disappear in the same way. We are there, then we are gone. But we don't go back fully into the void. Our flesh remains, that mass of molecules, of atoms, to be redistributed in the world. Perhaps there is less and less void ...

So I looked at my baby and was amazed at how much of a stranger he was, where before he had been a part of me: I had trouble realising that he was the same being, that he had simply separated from me. That we had separated from each other. The baby belonged to the world now, he was outside along with everything which was not me.

Then the nurse placed him at my breast. Where before I was overwhelmed with astonishment, I was now overwhelmed with love. I felt that, when I held him to me, I was like an animal. I would have turned fierce, I would have scratched, bitten, killed if anyone had tried to take him away from me. But nothing like that happened at the maternity hospital, and I eventually got very bored.

The first few hours in the Belltower I almost regretted the moments he was asleep. I wanted to touch him all the time, to hold him, to feel his little feet and his little hands, to kiss him, to pretend to eat him up.

Baby milk has a deliciously good smell. After I wash him my baby is the perfect cream puff.

You have to listen to newborn babies crying. They let out this little caterwauling which is simply adorable.

I love Johnny, of course. I who couldn't have a baby, before the bear. But sometimes I get tired of looking after him. I want him to be already grown up. So I go to see Omi, Gaël and Rachid at the Granary. Gaël has an old electric guitar he cobbled together himself, which he plays all the time, muted, his head bent over the neck as if he is in a world of his own. Omi is always on speed, he passes through with people we don't know and never see again, he fills Rachid in on the latest red-hot plan which is going to change their lives, and which never comes to anything. Rachid goes along with it, promises to do what Omi asks, to be at the rendezvous he sets up. I think he does it out of friendship, so as not to shatter Omi's eternal dream. But perhaps he believes in it himself, a little.

I'm in love with Omi, but it is virtually impossible to love him. He always has to go somewhere, he is never there, he gets on with everybody, but he escapes from them all, he escapes from me, I even think he escapes from himself, that he is never there in himself either.

The Granary is divided in two by a parachute hung between one wall and the other. Behind the curtain there is a mattress and a sheet. It is the lovers' bedroom of the Granary, where Omi and I go, or which Rachid uses when he is with a girlfriend. At night, on the other side, there are always people around, people Omi and

Rachid bring back. Joints are passed round, some harder stuff sometimes which I don't touch. When Omi wants me he takes me behind the parachute. Even when we are making love I don't know where Omi really is.

When Omi wants to see me he leaves messages on the walls of the church. Each morning I look to see if there is a new spray job. Sometimes he just writes 'Lucie', each time in a different colour or style. Or he draws a moon, a half-moon or a crescent moon. (He often calls me Moon or Moona, I don't know why. Omi never learned anything of his father's language, perhaps that's why he prefers to use the few English words that he knows. But I dream of hearing that language, which might tell me the truth about Omi, which might tell that truth to Omi himself. I dream about that language as of a distant land, a lost land where Omi lives. Omi who can't stay anywhere, not even in himself, Omi who always goes away . . .)

On other occasions he scrawled: 'I am looking for my light', 'the night is dark without my Lulu', 'where is the fairy?', 'come' . . . Sometimes there are obscene phrases or drawings. Omi says they aren't his, but I'm not so sure, so I go anyway. I like the fact that he asks me nothing when he takes me by the arm and leads me behind the parachute. I like responding to his messages in the church, even if they are perhaps not always from him. I'm not miserly with my love, and he knows it.

Omi has two white suits, always impeccably pressed, which he wears with brightly coloured tee-shirts, matching socks and polished, square-toed shoes. He goes about with his long, shiny, black hair tied back with a ribbon, his angelic head and his long silhouette, nonchalantly, like an eastern prince or an offbeat pimp. And me in my fuchsia-coloured pumps, my tight black dress and my enormous earrings, I look like a girl, a funny little girl, a bit gothic, striding around the streets and hanging around in cemeteries with a baby in my arms.

When I walk outside with Omi the town is no longer the same. The warm June air sparkles, vibrates and shatters into thousands of crystals lighter than bubbles. The people no longer have faces, the streets are suspended, I am hanging on Omi's look as he points out the rooftops, on Omi's mouth as he says that one day we will live in that huge apartment on the top storey, all covered with windows and a large veranda facing south-west. That it will have high ceilings, carpets, open doors connecting a suite of rooms. That on the side away from the street there will be a small window giving access to the rooftop. That Omi and Lucie will open the small window, that they will slip outside, and that they will make love on the warm tiles, in the light of the sky and the calls of the swifts.

In the mountains I went round naked. In town it is not possible to be undressed. Only in the abandoned church, where I wash, or on the rooftop, where Omi will take me one day. Even behind the parachute I never undress completely. I keep my stockings on. I don't think I will go entirely naked on the rooftop. The best thing would be to have a mask over my face.

From the Belltower I can see all the rooftops of the town. They form a huge formal garden, cut across by the dark straight veins of the streets, interrupted by the empty spaces of squares and cemeteries, by the modest napkins of gardens and parks, by the lofty landmarks of large monuments, spires and belltowers, and by the glass structures of Four Towers, at each corner of the Square. Further beyond, when there is no mist, all you can see is a strip of yellow or green. Above the rooftops the swifts streak the air with their sharp flights, slicing the sky with flashing ballets of black arrows.

The town is supposed to be divided into four quite distinct quarters. From my long observations in the Belltower I can't tell. There are no obvious dividing lines. Since no one knows where the quarters begin and end I don't know where to look for the borders. I search the complex geometry of sheet-metal, tiles, slates, chimneys, aerials, spires, skylights and domes, windows and walls, in all its perspectives, gradients, angles and corners, like someone trying to find the twelve constellations in the sky without ever having seen a map. Not that the town is uniform. Within its general harmony the town is so different at each moment, at each street corner, at each cluster of houses that I find it impossible, from the street as from the Belltower, to divide it into coherent units.

Omi makes out that the town has only two quarters. Other people claim there aren't any at all. I think that's going too far. I have often had the experience of passing from one quarter to another. To deny the existence of different quarters is to deny this experience of passing between quarters, which everyone has had. You are in the street when suddenly, mechanically, you push open the door of a building. You thought it was your dentist's, where you have an appointment, or the Social Security office, where you are due to drop off some papers, or even a dressmaker a friend had recommended . . . Whatever. You open this door and, instead of finding yourself in an entrance hall, a rather dark hallway where you would have reached out a hand for the timeswitch, instead of that you are back in a street, another street, a different street: wider, more open, with nicer buildings; or narrower, noisier, busier; or more of a shopping street . . . Anyway, you feel that you have entered a new quarter. But how? No one has ever been able to retrace their steps, nor return the same way another time. Once you are on the other side, you are immediately caught by the new street and you don't even give it any thought. And even if you made the effort to think about it, the time it takes to advance two or three steps, to turn back . . . and you never again find that door through which you entered. There is nothing for it but to take the first metro home. (It is obviously equally possible to move from one quarter to another on the metro; it is actually the commonest method, and the only one which is certain. But since the metro stays underground you don't always see where the quarters end.)

No one has ever explained the mystery of the façade-buildings, these false buildings which are nothing more than façades. In fact everyone, even those who insist on denying the existence of quarters, is familiar with this phenomenon, and no one really thinks about it any more. You are no more surprised than when you move from joy to pain, or from dreaming to waking, without exactly knowing through which door.

This afternoon, at the Captain's grave, I made the acquaintance of Nadia. Large black clouds were piling up over the wall of the cemetery. I saw her come in through the lower gate, enveloped in a flowing dress, which billowed in front of her, blown by the wind. I was in the middle of feeding Johnny, trying to shelter him at the same time. I too was struggling with the onset of the storm.

When she reached our level we exchanged a smile of complicity. Then she looked at the inscription on the stone and said: 'Ship's Captain! This is a wind worthy of him!' Then we began to talk.

She saw the round blue mark under Johnny's left ankle. I told her he had it at birth, that and the long, dark, silky hairs covering his back, which made the midwife gasp and put her in quite a disturbed state. I could see that Nadia wasn't sure whether I was joking, so I lifted up baby John's bodice and showed her. She was very impressed, like everyone. And like everyone, she made an effort not to show it.

I would like to know who this Captain was. Does it not bother him to be pinned down in the earth for evermore? Perhaps on the contrary this last voyage is the most adventurous he has ever known, perhaps he is navigating on board his coffin towards worlds we can't imagine . . . All the same, I pity him a little. He must have realised that his long voyage was not really all that long.

My bear also needed wide open spaces.

Where do bears go when they die?

I dreamed that the postman came to deliver a calendar. (In fact I never see the postman, since

I don't have a letter box. Who would write to me anyway? And I am not the sort who would have the post office calendar delivered.) The choice of photos caused me a few problems: cats in a basket, horses in a field, dogs, children and landscapes, all of which seemed to have no other purpose than to appear on a calendar which grandmothers could hang on the wall, next to the clock. Finally I chose a picture of a mountain (in spring on one side, in winter on the other).

Then the postman, who was a small man with a pointed face and greasy hair, stiff and awkward in his blue uniform, glanced around the Belltower and said to me with a sort of benevolent smile: 'They've done all this up. It's nice now.' And since I didn't want to appear uninformed I let him leave without asking for an explanation.

Then a young man turned up looking like a nineteenth-century poet, his shirt undone, thin, a feverish look in his eye and his hair blowing in the wind. He explained to me that he intended to create a wall newspaper. Would I allow him to borrow the wall of my church to stick up the literary texts of the great authors he had contacted (he gave me the names), who had expressed their enthusiasm for his idea, as well as the poems of a couple of his friends, as yet quite unknown to the general public, since they had never been published ('You know how the publishing systems works,' he added knowingly), whose enormous talent he had taken it upon himself to reveal.

I was just about to reply when the young man, glancing round the Belltower, added: 'I came here last year to see the flat which was for rent. In fact there were two flats here then.' 'I know,' I said, 'they got the builders in. They connected the two flats and now there's only one.'

When I woke up I looked at the Belltower to see if there was any trace of a former dividing wall. But the architecture of this church is so strange that it is difficult to find any certain indications. St Mark's is both unused and unfinished. It was built by a mad architect (possibly a genius) or an architect of genius (possibly mad), who died before bringing his work to completion. The plans for this neo-baroque basilica were so complex and so costly to realise that work on the church was halted after his death, even though it was nearly complete.

Half the roof is missing. The crane is still there, sticking up through the gap, standing as tall as the spire. It too had become etched over the course of time, worn by the sun, the rain, people's stares, and it now gives the impression of being part of the building.

For the first twenty-five years there were metal barriers around the church and a kiosk selling tickets to visitors wanting to see the unfinished monument. Then curiosity died down a bit, and a speculator had the idea of installing flats in those parts of the building which had four walls and a roof. He started with the Belltower, but his business began to fail and he abandoned the project. No one else took an interest in the ill-starred basilica, and I believe I am the first person in a period of nearly fifty years to squat in the flat, itself unfinished (it doesn't have any doors), which was installed in the Belltower.

Sometimes I feel there is something terrible trying to get out of me. It is not the mountain. I have disturbing dreams. For example: I have lions and tigers. They are constantly famished and roar in a monstrous way. I have to keep them supplied with quarters of zebra. They have incredibly voracious appetites and you have to feed them if you don't want them to devour you. Or another: the director of the zoo has brought the elephant into the swimming pool to show it to the children. He explains that he can't leave him there too long since his body heat causes the water temperature to rise quickly, and he would end up being boiled alive.

I feel like I am surrounded by signs I am unable to read.

I think it is the bear trying to get out. But who is he?

Pigeons strut and coo on the shiny red tiles. The rain has stopped. The sun has emerged from the clouds and is now hot. Steam rises from the tiles. I wish I were a cat so I could go walking on the rooftops.

When I was young I wanted to be everything I saw. I would see a cat with its bright eyes, its soft fur, its whiskers, its pink tongue and pointed teeth, and I would say: 'I want to be a cat.' I would climb the tree in the garden, stretch out on a branch and say: 'I want to be a tree.' I would pick up a pebble from the beach, all polished, salty and shiny from the sea, and I would say: 'I want to be a pebble.' I could already see that the world was entering into me through my desire; but also that I could not get outside of myself, really become a cat, a tree or a pebble.

In love the other enters into you, and in the pleasure of love you have the impression, briefly, of being outside yourself. But it is only through dying that you really leave yourself.

At the corner of the street the pâtissier has set up his ice cream machine, and his little assistant is handing out glorious Italian-style ice creams like inverted, static cyclones of smooth, glossy cream, ivory or brown, or the two mixed together, depending on whether you have chosen vanilla, chocolate or chocolate-vanilla. In front of me an old couple were waiting their turn, both frail and tottering, standing hand in hand: him, Dr Martens on his feet, khaki shirt and dark glasses; her, black gypsy skirt with flounces and a small fluorescent pink top tight over her free-hanging breasts. The most surprising thing was that in spite of her old, wrinkled, shrivelled apple of a face she had the breasts of a young woman, full and round. They were like two marvellous magical fruits, two peaches which forgot to fall and find themselves in mid-winter like two balls of light hanging incongruously on a bare tree – like a baby breastfeeding on a grave.

I wonder where I am. Why I followed the bear.

There is always tragic news in the papers. Just as the rain enters into me and forces me to flow out, so the world enters into me with all its beauty and all its tragedy. The world enters me at will for I am completely open, the world constantly subjects me to its influences, its order, while I, prisoner of myself, can do nothing to the world.

I feel that I am on the platform of a railway station, but I don't know which train I am waiting for.

I saw Nadia again. After our first meeting it began to rain, a long, fine, tightly packed rain which dragged on for days. I went back to the cemetery between showers and she was there. I was surprised, it was as if she were waiting for me. We walked together to the bottom of the cemetery, she held Johnny for me while I climbed the heap of faded flowers and old wreaths in search of pearls.

I had just finished when I felt the first drops of rain. 'Would you like to come back for some tea?' Nadia asked. 'I live quite nearby, and I'm on my own, my husband isn't there.'

Nadia lives quite near me, but on the other side of the cemetery. We debated whether it was the same quarter, but we didn't come to any firm conclusion. The front door of her building opens into a hallway, which leads to an interior court, open to the sky, a square, sad, grey little yard surrounded by walls five storeys high. Near a waterspout a little girl in a dress was squatting down and peeing on the concrete which was already damp from the rain, next to a mongrel which seemed to be bending over to keep an eye on the yellow puddle flowing gently down the slope.

Nadia tapped in her number, opened the grill and we climbed to the top floor. The wooden staircase smelled of polish; it was so shiny I was worried about slipping and falling with baby John. While Nadia was preparing the tea I looked at the courtyard through the kitchen window, listening to the sound of the water bubbling in the pan and of the rain beating against the windows.

'Life is not much fun here, is it?' Nadia said.

When I didn't reply she added: 'They say that outside the City life is different, less tiring, freer, more fun.'

'Then why don't you leave, or live some other way?' I said.

She turned her head and said quickly: 'You know it's not that simple.' And she brought the tray with the teapot, cups and some biscuits into the living room.

Nadia told me that she had been a doctor in a surgery for one year, since finishing her studies. She talked about her husband, who is an architect in a large office, and deplores the fact that no one in this town ever does anything new. She also made Johnny smile, and said that she hoped she could have a baby soon. I told her almost nothing about myself, but she seemed quite happy to have me listen to her.

I followed her into the kitchen when she took away the tea tray and I looked out of the window once again. The rain had stopped, the dampness left a little of its pale light on the concrete walls.

'What I like best in this town,' said Nadia, 'are the gardens. Especially the little ones, the squares hidden in the shadow of churches, or between two buildings, with only one or two seats. How is it that in the middle of town these squares manage to provide solitude and silence? It's a mystery I have never been able – in fact, never even tried – to explain, any more than the passageways and the façade-buildings. And I love the Central Library: concentrated dreaming. Concentrated time, as well . . .'

I kissed Nadia. We were now on first-name terms and we parted smiling.

Sometimes, during the day, I take my baby in my hands and, as if pretending to eat him, I unclench my jaws above his arms and I growl, I growl as deep a growl as I can manage, quite softly under my breath, like the distant cello of silence of the mountain.

How does time pass? Certainly not in a straight line, as we normally think. Otherwise why would the end be inscribed in the beginning? Time goes in a circle. Every being is a sort of atom of time, with an identity in the form of a nucleus and moments in the form of electrons. We imagine that we are free, that we have our life in front of us, and other such nonsense. Whereas we merely project ourselves, identify ourselves in a succession of moments, which simply revolve around us, combining with other moments in the world, incapable of changing their orbit.

Our lifespan depends on the time we take to do the tour of these moments. Some people choose a single moment in their orbit. They settle in, stay there for the time it takes this moment to make its journey around their nucleus, and they die. Others, seeing that they have a whole host of moments at their disposal, consumed with curiosity and desire, want to try everything: they leap from one moment to another, at the risk of sometimes going the wrong way, or of going too fast and arriving at the end of the journey sooner than expected. But perhaps it is just as dangerous to set off on a single moment: how do you know if it is a slow and careful moment, or one that will make you go round yourself in a flash?

The difficulty lies in not knowing in advance the character of the moments which carry you nor how they will bear up on their trajectory. And just when you think you are aboard one type of boat you may actually find yourself on board another.

*

You must obey yourself, listen to your nucleus.

Mankind is a troubled race, because they have discovered how to split the nucleus of the atom.

It is as though the bear is calling me, inviting me to free myself of the falsehood, the cowardice.

It is difficult to say anything when you risk splitting apart.

The bear stops me sleeping. I lie face down in my bed, the soles of my feet pressed against the end, my chin between my fists, staring at the white blot of the pillow.

I went to the Central Library. Nadia had warned me that entry was restricted to fully paid-up intellectuals. Four guards posted on each side of the two successive doors checked identities, searched bags, authorised access to the secretary's office and the cloakroom, then asked to see entry passes while searching the bags yet again. I pretended that I was a writer, and that I had to do research on twelfth-century Persia for my next novel. The lady in the secretary's office hesitated, then, reluctantly, agreed to give me a day pass, insisting that the next time I should bring along one of my publications.

At the entrance they handed me a square, white, translucent badge on which three black numbers were imprinted. I walked into the central bay, to the gangway where one of the tables bore the number which had been allocated to me: 413.

I switched on the round lamp which cast a flat light over the wood and sat down. I sat a while watching the people working around me, lines of heads lowered beneath lines of lamps, as if the heads and lamps were held at a fixed distance from one another by cosmic attraction, as if they were frozen in their gravity in such a way that you couldn't tell which sphere, the head or the lamp, was in orbit around the other.

The walls of the printed books room (which was huge, the biggest in the Central Library) were covered with four storeys of fat books with worn bindings. The uncertain white daylight fell from the windows in the ceiling, which was divided into supporting vaults by columns like some giant merry-go-round. In

front of the bookshelves were ranged four galleries edged by metal handrails, running round
the whole perimeter of the room, with narrow
stairways, tucked away deep in the recesses
like yawning mouths full of shadow, allowing
the librarians access to all the works. The end
of the room was in the shape of a huge hemi-
sphere, and along its curved wall was stacked
an even more staggering array of books. With a
cautious step I went up to the raised, crescent-
shaped counter where a man in an overall sat
and where there was an urn into which people
slipped rectangles of paper.

Up stairways, along corridors, I strode around
the Central Library, visited the periodicals
room, the Western and Eastern manuscripts,
the coins and medals, the maps and plans, the
stamps and photographs, the film and video,
the department of music and the record library.
Everywhere there were people, almost all of
them old, absorbed in reading or studying doc-
uments, and looking at them I wondered what
it was they were searching for.

When I got back to my seat I found that I
now had only one neighbour, an old gentle-
man with white hair, sitting with his back to
me.

'Excuse me miss,' he said.

He turned towards me.

'Ange Nardone. You were probably born too late, or too soon, to know me. For you books are antiques found only in museums like this, is that not so? Once there were places called bookshops, which regularly displayed in their windows my latest publications.'

I replied that I had read several books, when I was at school, and in particular one of his, *The White Cavalier*, I seemed to recall. Unfortunately I had no memory of any of my reading. It was as if the words entered my head and disappeared immediately, leaving only a vague impression. However, I still had a great curiosity for books. That is why I had come here today, to see them and smell them, which was a form of reading in itself.

I didn't dare to tell him that since it had been raining I had begun to write myself. I was thrilled to meet a writer, even if I couldn't remember whether he was an important author or not. We chatted a while longer, then he said in a somewhat muted voice: 'You remind me very much of a young girl I met in one of the rooms of this very library fifty years ago.'

Neither of us said anything. After a pause, he

added: 'It's . . . very strange.' Then we were silent again.

Finally, since he appeared confused, I asked him if he would like to tell me her story. I will try to record the exact words he spoke, in a low voice, late that afternoon in the almost deserted library.

'I met Lusi in one of the vast high reading rooms of the Central Library,' he said.

'For several months I had been conducting research on chthonic myths in popular stories, and every afternoon I consulted the fat French, English and German bibliographical indexes lined along the dozens of metres of shelves, opened countless drawers and card-indexes, checked international data banks on the computer, and borrowed rare scholarly works which the librarians carefully placed in my hands like fragile treasures.

'I had done a lot of work on myths of serpents, dragons and certain lunar divinities, and I had gathered together an important bibliography stretching from the Ancients to the modern day, from the Chinese to the Europeans, taking in the Persians, the Egyptians and the Aztecs. I had become interested in the chthonic horse, and had just finished studying *The Marvellous Adventures Underground and Elsewhere of Er-Toshtuk, the Giant of the Steppes* by Pertev Boratav. I began a more detailed study of the myth of Mélusine, which was leading me into more complex research than I had anticipated. After reading the novels of Jehan d'Arras and Couldrette I had followed in the steps of Jacques Le Goff and discovered the first images of Mélusine in the Latin literature of the twelfth and thirteenth centuries: in the *De Nugis Curialium* of Gautier Map, the *Super Apocalypsim* of Geoffroi d'Auxerre, the *Otia Imperialia* of Gervais de Tilbury, the *De Principis Instructione* of Giraud de Barri.

'Relatively few authors had been inspired by Mélusine: François Nodot, Joséphin Péladan, Vernon Lee, Franz Hellens had described her more obliquely or less successfully than Gérard de Nerval, Jean Lorrain or André Breton. But she had a strong influence on the popular imagination, which had rewritten her story a hundred times since the Middle Ages through the oral tradition, as witnessed by the folklorists Demaille, Dontenville and Kotte. However, I had found it impossible to record the essential representations of the serpent-woman, at least up to that afternoon, the day before I met Lusi, when I found out about a book, now probably destroyed, containing essential, hitherto unpublished, "marvellous and terrifying" information on Mélusine.

'From that point on I would concentrate my attention on the search for this lost image of the mythical creature through a close reading of a number of works, some of which, I hoped, must contain fragments, a trace, of this famous lost book.

'The light wood tables in the reading room were all occupied by students in shapeless dark clothes and a few lecturers in grey suits, their right hands resting on sheets of paper, pens encircled by index and middle fingers, while the fingers of their left hands were splayed to hold open books over which their heads were lowered, all this in a quiet, mouse-like buzz, a confused rustling of paper and whispered voices.

'Facing me a young, dark-haired girl, her face pink and smooth as if it had just been carefully washed with a flannel glove and soap, her hair discreetly pinned back by a tortoiseshell clip and falling on each side of her face behind her cheap earrings to her pearl-coloured cotton blouse, which was laced with embroidery in different shades of the same colour, buttoned up to the small round collar and half-hidden by a navy-blue sweater, with a cool mouth, finely drawn eyebrows, and her eyelids lowered on a curtain of eyelashes slightly thickened by a coating of mascara, a young dark-haired girl was resting her candid gaze and her small white hand with its fine gold-plated rings on a fat old book, which lay open in the middle, unfolding two weighty wings with a span wider than that of her narrow chest.

'Even though I was myself busy reading a book almost as bulky I couldn't resist looking up at regular intervals at this enchanting image. After three weeks of uninterrupted rain the town was beginning to breathe gently in a radiant April light. Through the windows of the large bays at the end of the room a soft sky the colour of babies' clothes began to turn blue against the pale stone and slate roofs of the church and the adjacent presbytery. Outside the streets were full of the scents of buds, and women went out without overcoats, light and smiling. I had had a dismal winter, divided between work, boredom and evenings spent with friends intended to fill my solitude. But the return of fine days, the ever stronger smells of spring in the streets as I walked to the library each afternoon, the serenity of the sky above the rooftops, the stream of soft light above my table, this young dark-haired girl opposite me, leaning so gracefully over her book, all this invited me to hope, to move, to love, to live.

'However, in spite of the noiseless atmosphere of the place, in spite of my good humour and my new-found confidence, the dull anxiety which had taken hold of me the previous evening did not relent. I had run up against an enigma, I had lost the thread which till then had guided my research along tracks which, though not devoid of surprises, were always verifiable. Suddenly that hitherto familiar universe of ordered, filed, classified texts had become, through the appearance of a single anomaly, like a jungle of masked words whose meaning was hidden.

'By chance, while flicking through the AUTHORS card index, my attention was caught by the title of a book which neither the bibliographies nor the SUBJECTS card index mentioned: *The Cries of the Fairy*.

'It was an eighty-page leatherbound octavo, signed by Campbell Saint-Clair. Although it contained no mention of either the place or date of publication, it was easy to work out, from the appearance of the book and the style of the author, that it must have been written and published in the second half of the nineteenth century – especially since the title of the book was evidently a reference to the last few words of the final alexandrine of the poem *El Desdichado*.

'In an introduction, where he announced that what he was about to narrate was his own "entirely truthful" story, Campbell Saint-Clair presented himself as the last descendant of a great ruined family, living alone on a modest pension in a small flat in the Rue de Seine where, in between nights of merrymaking in the company of rowdy comrades and jolly actresses, he tried to cultivate his talents as a poet. On one such afternoon, when he had woken up still jaded by the excesses of the previous evening he decided, as was his wont, to gather his wits and search for inspiration on a long walk through the town.

'"It was the end of March," he wrote. "The sun had emerged from the thick grey clouds and flooded with its warm light the pavements still damp from recent rain. I felt a sweet *joie de vivre* growing within me, as if the new Spring which was breaking out over the town was also working its way into my heart. Standing amidst the people out strolling on the Pont des Arts I looked down over the Seine. I then crossed to the right bank and sauntered around for a long time.

'"I regretted once more having spent a whole night indulging in facile pleasures, and as I walked along I promised myself to give up this dissolute existence and devote myself henceforth to the work which I bore within me, the great poem which would show to the world the depth and beauty of my tortured soul. Already verses, rhymes, metaphors were springing to mind, and I was so enraptured that I was pulled up short by the dark wall at the end of a blind alley, not knowing by which network of streets I had found my way to this silent deserted place.

'"At this very moment the rain began to fall. I glanced at the sky and saw that the clouds had turned black. Lowering my gaze I saw in the window of the sinister building which closed off the alley a white shape which arrested my attention. A young woman of great beauty, dressed in white, huge eyes in her pale face surrounded by long hair, stood framed in the casement, motionless, her hands against the pane. I thought I could see tears rolling down those alabaster cheeks. I entered the . . ."

'The story stopped there, broken off at the bottom of page 13. Twenty-seven pages had been torn out. On page 40 Saint-Clair was wandering from villages to châteaux, from châteaux to forests, though it wasn't clear what the object of his quest was. He described each place (in Aunis, Provence, the Hainaut, Bourbonnais, Champagne, the Jura, the Aube, the Côte-d'Or, the Drôme; as well as the châteaux and towns built by the fairy: Lusignan, of course, but also Parthenay, Saint-Maixent, Talmont, Linges, Pons, Vouvant, Mervent, Melle, in the Vendée) for page after page, in poetic profusion, lamenting and exalting in his solitude and his dissatisfaction. Finally he returned to Paris, crossed the Seine a second time, and set off in search of the blind alley which he had chanced upon the first time. He went into the building and opened the door leading to the room.

'The room was empty except for a table on which lay an "ancient book" bound in shagreen with long golden spirals on the cover, a book containing "marvellous and terrifying revelations on the fairy Mélusine", indicating "signs scattered throughout the world, in the sight of all, yet which no one can see, which prove the existence of her powers, her manifestations and her incarnations, her eternity and her ubiquity". These revelations were of a nature such that Saint-Clair, believing himself both chosen and cursed, saw it as his duty to destroy the book, "so that it will never again illuminate nor annihilate the life of any human being" after him, and so that Mélusine, for whom he declared his "eternal love", would not be "threatened by human knowledge of her existence, of her true nature". Campbell Saint-Clair ended by announcing his departure for the mountains, where he intended to live out his days as a hermit so as to be "nearer to the fairy" who had "shown him the secrets of the world, opened to him the gates of happiness and sorrow," the better to "cherish her and remain true to her".

'Although the author seemed in a state of excitement, there was nevertheless a tone of sincerity in this detailed account (although the details were unfortunately attached to the least important elements in the story), a tone which lent it the force of authenticity, in spite of the ardour, the naivety and the infelicities of a patently over-emotive mind. That Campbell Saint-Clair had greatly exaggerated the nature of the revelations I had no doubt; but I was equally convinced that his text was no joke, that he had indeed lived the story which he recounted (and which unfortunately lacked an important section owing to the pages that were torn out), that he had indeed found and read this ancient book, and that what was written in this book was influential enough to cause a young poet to exclude himself from the world and go to live among the beasts of the mountains.

'And I now realised, in the soft murmur of the library, as the young dark-haired girl closed her satchel and left her seat, that this old, irrecoverable book still had the power, a century after its disappearance, to arouse my curiosity and exert such an influence on me that my thoughts returned to it incessantly, that underlying all my actions, all my reflections, all my feelings, even the most mundane, something spurred me on incessantly, some kind of terrifying *desire for knowledge*.

'Wearing pumps, sheer light-coloured stockings which clung tightly to her perfectly shaped legs, a supple aquamarine outfit tailored in shimmering silk moving with the long lines of her body, Lusi approached with a light, graceful step, radiant and reserved, her skin a dazzling white rendered even more luminous by the red line of her fleshy lips and the mass of hair with its russet sheen, falling free in waves to her shoulders.

'When she sat down opposite me in the seat just vacated by the fresh-faced student, the old-fashioned smell of wood, of paper, of the open satchels and the grey overalls of the librarians disappeared beneath the warm breath which floated around Lusi, a fragrance, both tonic and sickly, of sap and berries with a faint, barely discernible scent of dead leaves: a discreet smell yet one as brutal as it was sweet, a smell of undergrowth which intoxicated me and rendered me numb.

'Lusi sat motionless like a marble statue, her pupils instantly closed to a pinpoint in the centre of her cold green irises, her eyes, like almond-shaped slits, fixed on some point on the shelves while I looked at her, my heart seized with wonder, petrified at finding, after days and days of research through thousands of yellowed pages, dozens of worn books, through centuries past, forgotten legends and dead authors, petrified at finding in front of me this strangely beautiful woman, this silent unfeeling presence like that of a dream or an apparition.

'Some minutes later, Lusi got up to collect the book she had ordered from the counter. When she returned we struck up a conversation. This was the first time she had come here, she told me. She had felt a sudden desire to reread a book which had made her cry a lot as a child. She wanted to know whether that emotion had changed with time. She laughed as she said it, but I thought I could see tears in her eyes. It was exactly the same book as the one from her childhood, she said, as she turned the pages, with the same black-and-white photos.

'The last picture showed a white horse with a small boy on its back, forging through the water of a grey river. Lusi read the final lines. I saw her lips tremble. Then she lowered her

head and started crying silently. I reached out
my hand towards hers, slowly, with great effort,
animated and paralysed by desire and fear,
touched softly the ends of her fine white fingers
and in a whisper offered to take her home.

'Lusi lived in the château of the White Lady at
the gates of the city. It was an old square-
shaped building, well known in the region,
flanked by a round tower where Lusi had
arranged her room. It was protected from view
by an untended, overgrown park surrounded by
high railings covered with vegetation which
grew thicker and thicker as the summer
approached – brambles, long nettles, great
clumps of arums and rhododendrons – and
dripping with ivy, Virginia creepers and convol-
vulus, joined in places by the branches of weeping willows.

'Her mother, whom she never knew, had
left her this house in her will, along with
several acres of woodland which was main-
tained and exploited for the production of
paper pulp. Lusi had no father nor any family.
She had been raised by two servants who still
lived in an apartment on the ground floor. One
of them, who dressed habitually in black

trousers and sweater, did the gardening and other odd jobs. She was small and excessively thin, but whenever she put on shorts and a tee-shirt when working in hot weather she revealed her fine, flawless skin, her firm muscles, her tapering legs and her arms which showed no sign of sagging in spite of her age. The quiet type, she avoided meeting people and flitted among the trees like a shadow. Larger and rounder, her companion was affable and always smiling, to the point of appearing a bit simple. When she wasn't busy in the kitchen, she wandered the corridors of the château, a vacuum cleaner or bucket in her hand, wrapped in a white apron. Where the park had its dark phantom, the house was patrolled by her pale silhouette, to the gentle clinking of household utensils.

'Lusi had grown up alongside these two women in complete freedom. "If only you could have seen how beautiful they were when they were young," she said. "I would so much love to look like them! To have Nine's dark eyes and slim build, or Noune's red lips and round breasts! When I was little I climbed on Nine's knees and she told me fairy stories. The fairies had great adventures and accomplished marvellous feats in their own kingdom and the kingdom of men. But men became enamoured of them, and they of men, and they always ended up unhappy victims of love. I would draw Noune towards us, bury my face in her soft breast and say: "I will always stay with you, I will never love any man." And Nine and Noune would cradle me, and give me a piece of cake and a glass of warm milk."

'The day Lusi told me this story I thought I understood that the condition she placed on our love originated in these old wives' tales, in that childhood bathed in a vague fear of men. Alas, I was later to discover that Lusi's difference, far from being the mere effect of a nervous disorder, a mere psychological block, was quite real. Lusi in love behaved in a peculiar way because she *was* peculiar.

'As a teenager Lusi discovered she had a talent for building. When the house was in danger of falling into ruin she drew up renovation plans, hired workmen, oversaw their activities. As part of the work she had a separate apartment constructed for the two old dears, and a bathroom in the centre of the hearth, hidden behind the doors of a large chimney.

'"Building a house is a fine thing," she said. "Often it begins with a sacrifice: first of all you need to cut down the trees on the site. Later the house breathes the ghostly breath of the felled trees it is resting upon. They sigh with sorrow during the night; that is why the house creaks when everything is supposed to be asleep. It sometimes happens that the stunted roots need to stretch themselves a bit; and so, without knowing why, you see the house begin to crack from the force of their contractions. Then one day, the day when they really need to loosen up, to get comfortable, to squirm in their root-like way, that day all the cracks, visible and invisible, in a mood of celebration or anger, join up in one huge zigzag, and the house collapses.

'"So you build another one elsewhere. First the foundations. It's rather like the way in which male animals urinate to mark the limits of their territory: see that layer of concrete, marked out by string, that's my place; from now on anything which goes up inside this perimeter will be in some way part of me, and I dare you to enter without being invited. Then you erect the walls, stone by stone, brick by brick, as if space were a giant puzzle whose gaps must be filled, piece by piece. Emptiness is unbearable, isn't it? At this point the house looks a bit scary: like a childbirth in process it is neither pretty nor clean. It doesn't yet have a human form, so to speak, the materials are still on view, spread out all over the place, the workers sweat in the hot sun to give it some of their souls.

'"It is no use having a horror of gaps, you need them for the doors and windows. That's how thieves get in, in spite of your warning string around the foundations, just as other thieves get into you through the gaps of your eyes, even though you never invited them in. But you have to have an opening to the world if you want to breathe.

'"Now, with its four walls and the gaps for the doors and windows the house looks exactly like a skull. It's already more human. My ancestors live in my head, I can live in the head of my ancestors. Now it is time for the magnificent ballet of the carpenters. Raising a roof is something else entirely from raising walls. You can't just pour in a mass of concrete. You aren't on the ground any more, you are almost touching the sky. You've got to be equal to it: aereate. You weave a net of beams, you return to the sky the branches you took from it, but now ordered, structured, cut, thought out.

'"You feel a little like an animal tamer; the creature has been captured, tamed, you can happily close the cage and put on the roof. The rest is about refinements, the finer details for making life comfortable: installing the nervous system of wires and pipes which will bring water, light and warmth, pointing, plastering, carpeting, wainscoting and glazing ... The house is divided up like a clock, with spaces for the hours of sleep, others for mealtimes, for washing, resting, receiving and getting together ... And small spaces for small moments, like taking off your coat when you come in, for example.

'"And other spaces again which no one sees, and which belong to the internal time of each person in the house: the baby, the father, the mother, the adolescent. For each of them the space inside the house has a different design.

'"But that doesn't really interest the builder any more. His work is done. From the outside the house simply looks like a comma. Rows of houses are like rows of commas. The time of a family, comma; the time of a family, comma;

etc. There are no doubt words inside the houses, but you don't know what they are. Writers come by and act all extra-perceptive; they make sentences out of all the words you can't see and all the commas you can.

'"There are more well-to-do houses whose time is supposed to last longer; they are like semi-colons. My house, this château which one of my ancestors built, resembles ellipses . . ."

'As I wanted to finish my work as soon as possible we didn't see each other for a few days. But at night I would go to bed and try to conjure up the image of her naked body. It never worked, and my desire was exasperated. I would think "she is mad", and then immediately afterwards "it's only a game, she only wants to play". But neither solution satisfied me. I thought about not seeing her again, but that was unbearable. In my fury I planned to burst in upon her and undress her before she had the chance to open her mouth. I wore myself out imagining this scene, and I finally fell into a sleep interrupted by erotic dreams and nightmares.

'I had a rendezvous with Lusi, but each of my steps was so slow, so heavy that hours passed, days passed, and I knew I was never going to arrive. Or else, I found her lying in a clearing at night, in the moonlight, with several naked men; sometimes she was fully dressed and lavished lustful kisses on each of them; sometimes she was naked, but covered with the hands and bodies of the men massed around her. I tried to cry out but no sound escaped my lips. I advanced, brandishing a knife, but just as I was about to plunge it into her flesh she vanished, and the men's bodies vanished also. I woke up in a sweat.

'Another time she had a pale, angelic face, surrounded by a halo of light. She opened her blouse, revealing her little breasts, round and white. She was walking forward through the park of the château, between the hanging curtains of the weeping willows. Now she moved away; I ran after her, caught her, pushed her over onto the grass, lay on top of her. Then I felt a terrible biting pain in my chest. She had sunk her teeth into my heart and was eating it! I opened my eyes, leapt out of bed, with a painful tightness in my chest.

'At the library I spent hours reading all the works where there was the merest chance of finding an allusion to the book destroyed by

Saint-Clair, but my work remained fruitless. And, little by little, I gave up hope of ever knowing the truth of this story. Especially since, after a few days of solitude, an overwhelming desire to see Lusi again got the better of my nightly torments and the difficulties of my work.

'Lusi often followed Nine out into the park. They could be seen together, leaning over the beds, wandering among the willows.

'At the end of the park, in the middle of a tangled, overgrown garden, abundant in plants and flowers, a fountain plashed in a stone basin. Lusi took me there one day. She pushed through the brambles and red poppies as if entering a temple. She looked tenderly at the thorny stems, saying, "At the end of August they will be covered with big, dark, sweet blackberries. There is no better fruit. They crunch and melt at the same time in your mouth, and each of their bursting seeds spreads over your taste buds all the sap gathered secretly by their untouchable branches. Brambles, I kiss your eyes.' She brushed the poppies with her legs, and whispered to them also her declarations of love. It was as if she had regressed to her childhood, and I wasn't sure whether I was touched or embarrassed.

'She sat down beside the fountain, gazed at her reflection a long time, then she slipped her ring from her finger and dropped it into the water. Feigning despair she demanded, as if proposing some terrible test, that I put my hand in the water to retrieve the silver ring which otherwise she never removed from her left hand. Then suddenly comforted, and apparently a little confused by her own childish behaviour, she kissed me passionately. Blackbirds sang in the trees around us, the water flowed, Lusi smelled of wild spice.

'Before we left the garden she knelt down for a moment to scratch the earth with her nails, the same as she had done a few days earlier on an outing to the beach with some friends of ours. Lying on her stomach in the sand she had begun playing with the grains, as you do, pouring them from one hand to the other. But she got so involved in her game that she forgot about us entirely. With staring eyes, the pupils closed in the centre of her green irises like when we first met, she whistled random notes between her teeth. Then she made off towards the damp sand in a crawling movement of surprising speed. Some of us were standing round chatting, others were lying on their towels with their eyes closed, soaking up the first rays of sunshine. No one paid any attention to her – I made sure of that when I saw her crawl off in that way.

'Having dug a well in the wet sand until she found water, Lusi started to build a castle surrounded by a moat. She worked diligently, modelling turrets, ramparts, a bridge, gates, loopholes. Some children had gathered round, and were surrounding her buildings with trenches and sandpies.

'In the lake Lusi quickly outstripped the best swimmers among us. She disappeared under the water, resurfacing far ahead. In the end we lost sight of her completely, and we had been back on the beach for ages when she came out of the water, dripping like a water-sprite in her silver bathing costume.'

Closing time had arrived. I asked Ange if he wanted to come back with me to finish his story at home. Before we went down into the metro I noticed on several buldings long lizards which I had never seen before.

We called at Nadia's to pick up Johnny, then we went back to the Belltower.

The sun was setting in a dreadful red sky. As the old man continued his story we sat watching the long strips of cloud stretched across the town, inflamed like shreds of flesh.

'We were married at the end of June,' he continued.

'Lusi was resplendent in her long white sheath. She danced well into the night, her head a little bent back, her eyes shining, her mouth open in a broad, unbroken smile. I led her in a last waltz. She seemed intoxicated by the music, by the swirling of our bodies. She held her leg tightly pressed between mine, she arched her back. She had a swooning look about the face which made her eyelids heavy and puffed up her now more softly smiling lips.

'The guests departed, a few hangers-on lay snoozing in the chairs around the ballroom. I took Lusi by the hand and we disappeared together into the corridors of the château. Our footsteps echoed in the dark. We walked in the silence without looking at each other, either too afraid or too impatient. At the foot of the stairs I held her by the shoulders against the wall.

Slowly she slid down to the floor with me. I held her on top of me, crouched on my lap, her legs wide, her stomach against mine. My head in her breasts I closed my eyes and gently grabbed her ankles and slid my hands up inside her dress. My chest was tight with emotion. I felt as if I was close to a priceless treasure, but one which I could never take possession of. Warm and throbbing next to me, reeling with love, Lusi seemed like a land where I would never arrive, a far off, miraculous spring which would transform into a mirage as soon as you lowered your mouth to quench your thirst.

'Lusi pressed her stomach against mine. I took her in my arms, carried her up the stairs to our bedroom.

'Long dark tapestries of watered silk hung in the windows. I lay my wife on the bed and lifted up her dress. Above her stockings her naked pale thighs and, beneath the white lace, the dark triangle of her sex. I wanted to raise the dress higher on her stomach but she gestured to me to stop. Suddenly I slipped her pants over her suspenders, lay on top of her, penetrated her, took her urgently, desperately, without a sound. We reached a brutal climax.

*

'The room rippled imperceptibly with the shimmer of inky black and silver. The heavy curtains, touched by the gleam of the moon, blended into the thick shadow inside. The room had a high ceiling, its furniture was adapted to its circular shape: an ebony table, a huge concave wardrobe in polished wood, a couch and two armchairs covered with dark moire. The deep four-poster bed was fitted with sheets cut from an old, fine ecru linencloth and two square-shaped pillows. Paintings of symbolist inspiration, with darkly reflecting surfaces, were hung on the walls. There were Salomés in the style of Gustave Moreau, cruel and precious scenes, painted in fine detail and set in décors strangely similar to that of our room. On the table a pot-bellied vase containing a bunch of white, open roses, already wilting slightly in the heat and emitting a stale smell.

'At the end of the room, opposite the bed, the wall was almost entirely occupied by a huge chimney breast, closed off by two iron doors, over which was hung the same watered silk which covered the windows and the seats. Behind the chimney breast Lusi had installed her bathroom, which I was forbidden to enter. I later discovered the perfumed jewel case behind the dark doors, filled with bottles and completely devoid of mirrors.

'I came out of the shower and went back to the room through the dark corridor. Lusi was still locked away in the chimney breast; I could hear sounds of running water. I went over to the tapestries, opened them a chink. There were curtains of white muslin hanging behind the dark silk. I pulled them round behind my head. They closed behind me with a rustle, and, standing there before the window, I felt as if I had penetrated Lusi's bridal veil. I saw her again as she left the church, looking straight and serious as she emerged from the veil held up by her maids of honour – much too serious for the photographer, who was forced to ask her to smile. Although I tried to put this lack of spontaneous joy down to the emotion of the occasion, the episode made me feel ill at ease.

'I opened the window and felt on my face the gentle breeze of a fine summer's night. The park glimmered softly. The weeping willows slowly swung their long arms along the ground, rustling quietly as their leaves rubbed together, casting thin trails of light against the lawn. The freshly mown grass seemed to exude the intimate scent of a woman, a vast woman, whose skirts were the curtains rippling against me, heavy and fluid, whose underclothes, shimmering with shadows and milk, I had penetrated, whose body smelled sweet, whose body was everywhere, but ever invisible, untouchable.

'The silken doors of the chimney breast opened. Lusi had put on a white silk nightdress and had unfastened her hair.

'I was struck by her beauty, as if she were appearing to me for the first time. "So this is the woman you love," I said to myself. And, almost timidly, I went up to her, took her face in my hands and pressed my lips to hers.

'I wanted to lead her to the bed, but she noticed the open window and leant over to look outside. I couldn't see her face. "The moon is up," she said. The moon was on the other side, behind her head. She turned towards me. Her eyes were inordinately wide. She dropped to the floor, where she stretched out full length on her stomach and began to kiss my feet passionately.

'I was used to Lusi's odd changes of mood when we were alone. But I was still somewhat taken aback. Her kisses were damp, I knew that she was crying. I wanted to lift her up. I desired her, I wanted to carry her to the bed, to take her, to console her. She prevented me. She got up onto her haunches, made me kneel down and move back to the foot of the bed, spread my arms in a cross and closed my hands around the brass pillars.

'The light of the moon, flowing in through the open window, lit up half of her face where her tears still glistened and fell onto the breast which was now hanging out of her nightdress. On the side of her face which was plunged in shadow I could only make out the gleam of her eye. "I shouldn't have done it," she said. "You must forgive me." She repeated "you must forgive me". Then she lowered her head over my stomach and didn't move.

'There was a dull cracking in the walls and I thought of the story which Lusi told me about the roots which try to stretch out under the foundations. A kiss which contained a threat. Her feverish kiss, as I knelt against the foot of the bed. And her, in the white nightdress which was slipping off her shoulders, the well of shadow between her breasts, the dark mass of her lowered head, her hair glistening in the moonlight. Her, drinking me in, humble and ardent, her dark look, her exaggerated smile, her scent, her shining eyes, her buttocks, her mouth, her fear, her look. Her way of kissing my neck like she would a child's, her silent supplication, as if to her lord and master.

'Far away, so far I thought I was dreaming it, there was a sound of footsteps, scarcely audible yet constant. The double veil fluttered in front of the open window, casting moving arabesques on the polished surface of the tall wardrobe. Gradually the sound of the footsteps became clearer and louder until they finally stopped outside the door, then started off again and faded away. It was a slow shuffling step, the step of Noune. What was she doing in the corridors at the dead of night? I strained my ear, but heard nothing but the groans of the stones and floorboards.

'Was it from passing my first night in this château which in daylight I found so light and comely? An insidious fear began to rise from the depths of my breast. I thought I heard the footsteps again. Sometimes I thought there was someone walking in the attic over our heads, sometimes that someone was pacing out the tiles in the passage and the kitchen on the ground floor. In the end I could not be sure that I was really hearing these footsteps at all.

'I hadn't as yet opened all the doors in the château. I was enclosed as in a woman's belly, dark, teeming with mysteries, laments and desires, haunted by a jealous old woman, who sighed as she dragged her fat legs, awaiting the day when she will get back her lovely dark-haired child, now lying in the marriage bed, offered in sacrifice to the man, the old enemy, the killer of fairies. Don't women prefer other women? Do they ever tire of adoring their bodies, their curves, their softness, their plenitude, their engulfing violence? What man could ever fill the endless expectation of women, the exhausting, monstrous expectation of women?

'I still wonder sometimes why I fell in love with Lusi. It is difficult to believe in chance when you are in the grip of love. There is something so incomprehensible and so luminous in the revelation of shared love that you can't help feeling chosen by providence.

'Perhaps I loved Lusi in order to go with her to the end of that night, to see what I shouldn't have seen, and to write these words today.

*

'Lusi's incomprehensible demands became on this wedding night an ordeal of doubt and pain. As she lay waiting next to me on the bed where I had carried her I looked at her face in the hope of finding, if not an explanation, at least a familiar expression which might afford me some reassurance. At that moment she slowly turned her head into a pale ray of light reflected by the wardrobe. The forms of the tapestries, now reduced to a faint shadow, began to play across her face; her features seemed fragmented, unstable, changing according to the rhythm of the gentle rippling of the curtains. She breathed without a sound and waited.

'Lusi was at home. And I was in a place which was completely foreign to me. I had just married a woman who was completely unknown to me, a woman from nowhere who imposed her whims upon me. I was going to live in this house which was nothing other than her own reflection and where I would never recognise myself. My heart was gripped with anguish, I wanted to escape. Was I not made for adventure, travel, the easy life of a young man with so many experiences, so many countries, so many women even still ahead of him?

'I turned towards Lusi, lying beautiful and calm on her back beneath the white silk pulled up over her sex, calm, only just given away by the glint in her eyes, beneath the white silk, in the chiaroscuro of the room attached to her form like a second shining skin, a fine, diaphanous skin as if shed by a snake in the depths of the bushes. Her way of pulling off her tight gloves, worn elbow-length and puckered at the wrist. The leather boots moulded around her feet and ankles, her dresses tight on her hips . . .

'In a moment I would place my mouth on her thigh and she would open up to me. And, as long as I delayed the moment, I would feel dizzy with the tension of my desire, the magnificent physical proof of my wish to possess this woman and, through her, her whole domain, which, once subjected, would feel in its entrails the proof of my power and my virility.

'That insistence they have in asking you, without even saying anything, for these "I love you"'s, and the proof of these "I love you"'s. That perpetual dissatisfaction, that hunger, that need to hoard you in your entirety, like a child they want to fill their bellies with. That sailor's wife mentality, standing constantly on the quayside, watching the cycle of tides, of the moon, watching the sea, their sister and rival, the gigantic devourer of men. How could they be satisfied with only one man? Their thirst for love is equalled only by their treachery. Those glints of appetite in Lusi's eyes when she talked to a man ... That way they have of feigning indifference, while letting you know they will stop at nothing, from one moment to the next, with the bewildering speed of a spider on its web, leaping towards the insect after hours of immobility ... Both Penelope and Célimène at the same time. Weaving cloth, to fill up their waiting hours, whose threads are men and whose weft is seduction.

'It was I who betrayed her. I see that now. Although reduced to a few hours, the night was still too long not to eat away at my trust. But doubt had taken hold of me much earlier, when I discovered that the woman I had fallen in love with, smiling, self-confident, dominating men with her charm, was not the same woman who slept in my bed, strange and capricious, with her mark of interdiction, exaggeratedly submissive, devoted to my body, which made her tremble with the desire, exacerbated by her self-imposed abstinence, to wrap herself in love to the point of suffocating me – or suffocating herself.

'I turned towards Lusi. Her eyes were wide open and she looked at me with a barely perceptible smile. With an unflinching expression of ecstasy and expectancy, she stared into my eyes as though she could see behind them. Then she looked at my body and reached out her hand towards me. I stroked her legs from her feet to her hips, slid my head between her thighs. In the shadows of her flesh I smelled the damp, freshly-dug earth. She began to sigh, moan, arch her back. Deep thicket where I would gladly bury myself forever, which she opened and opened and strained urgently to where her pleasure willed her.

'When I returned to her and kissed her she flared her nostrils like an animal and shuddered, intoxicated by the smell of her own body on my face. She drew me towards her and lost me from view, her eyes closed with full intensity on the interior of herself.

'The breeze had dropped, there wasn't a breath of air. The rustling of the leaves and the curtains, and all the sounds of the house had stopped. Only the sound of our breathing resonated in the silence.

'I was hot. My skin rubbed against the cloth folded over Mélusine. She was clinging to my back, her head bent back in pleasure.

'Her eyes still closed.

'Beautiful.

'Exciting.

'I took the white silk between my fingers, raised it over her stomach.

'Then Lusi, Lusi who just now had crawled at my feet, she, she who cried, and spoke, she, my gentle little black cat, my love, her velvet eyes, Lusi's eyes, shining, my two small lights in the shadows, who will light up the dark now?

'then Lusi, my beautiful one, with silver traces on her cheeks, why are you crying, my little Lusi, don't cry, my Lusi, I wanted to love you, I didn't know, don't cry any more, Lusi, your tears cause me so much pain, I hear them rising from the lake, they are like the lament of dead water but I know it is you, Lusi,

'then Lusi, who gave me her breasts in the moonlight, her white thighs in the moonlight, Lusi, whose buttocks are like moons, two beautiful full moons, she whose look pierced your heart like in ancient stories, Lusi who now moans in the lake, who vomits sand, hidden behind the yellow reeds, is it you, Lusi?

'then Lusi, my only love, the woman, the only one, who had been with me so long, waiting, Lusi who talked, who talked and was silent in the shadow, until I kiss her, Lusi,

'what is this story about, Lusi, I don't understand,

'then Lusi, you know, who loved to crawl over my stomach, between my legs, wrap herself around me, you might have been able to keep her, you, such a loving woman, you would have believed her, you wouldn't have been impatient, curious, foolish like me, you would have understood how important it was, you would have said yes to her and you would not have worried about it again, because you would have asked for it, since she would have given you almost everything of herself, since she would have given you all the rest, you would have seen that she was right, that you can't see everything, have everything, know everything, you would not have let her get away, Lusi, Lusi, who so loved to dance, to laugh, to love me,

'then Lusi, you see, Lusi, I have trouble

saying it, yet I swear that it didn't matter, I still loved you, even after I saw I loved you, I loved you even more,

'then Lusi, whom I held so often in my arms, held so tight against me, Lusi whose hair smelled so good, Lusi who had such strange, such delicious ways in bed, who opened her big eyes to look at me, who meditated so gravely before my sex as if before the mirror of her fountain, murmuring forthright, childish words of love, even more heartfelt than her declarations to the brambles and the poppies, Lusi who so loved pleasure and kissed the trees till her eardrums trembled, Lusi who dreamed of rivers and said that she would be my river of ink,

'then Lusi, my white and sombre one,

'Lusi whom I saw bent over her paper when she wrote poems for me,

'Lusi who leaned over the waters, dug the earth with her fingers and raised castles,

'who yielded between my hands,

'who trembled beneath her veil,

'and cried on her wedding night,

'Then Lusi opened her eyes, let out a long cry and pulled the cloth back over her stomach.

'Her emaciated stomach, from which had sprung a monstrous scaly mass, a long, wide, horrific scar incrusted deep into the wizened skin stretched between the jutting bones, coiled into her skin like a serpent whose head was rising up towards her throat between her skeletal ribs.

'She ran to the window with harrowing cries of despair, cries the like of which I had never ever heard, agonising cries from the depths of her stomach.

'I didn't have the strength to go to her and take her hand. I didn't have time to see her jump or fall. She disappeared.

'Finally I went to the window, called her, tried to make out the shape of her body on the lawn. Dawn was breaking, but the light was blocked out by a pall of black smoke which carried the strong smell of burning wood. I ran down the stairs, naked, crossed paths with Nine and Noune, who turned to follow me out into the park, beneath the window of our room.

'We never found Lusi. How could she have got away after her fall, how could she evade our searches which lasted all day and continued long after that? That first day I and the two women, later aided by neighbours and friends, scoured the whole park and the surrounding area, which was now covered by an opaque blanket of acrid smoke which irritated our eyes and throats. A violent blaze had taken hold of the huge forest which lay not far from the château. In my despair I felt as if the world were coming to an end, and I kept stopping to weep at my misfortune, and that of Lusi and that of the trees.

'I left the château, the lake and the forest, and moved into town. Having discovered in Lusi's bathroom an ancient book, bound in shagreen, with long golden spirals on the cover, whose pages were all blank, I shut myself away for good. Racked with grief, I began to write.

'Sometimes I think that Lusi is guiding my hand, that my books are children which she gives me. And, at night, I thank her and ask her forgiveness.'

It was now completely dark. The wind shunted the dark mass of cloud; a crescent moon appeared now and again, and the occasional solitary star. In the dark I looked at the handsome, sad face of the old writer, his solid features, his thick white eyebrows, his prominent cheekbones, his small shining eyes. I remembered that I reminded him of Lusi, and I invited him to spend the night with me.

First of all I heard Johnny moaning, a strange whine like a distressed animal. Then I felt the tremor, the merest tremor of an enormous force, accompanied by a low, distant rumbling which seemed to come from the belly of the earth. Then the sirens began to wail.

I leapt out of bed, took baby John in my arms, and ran downstairs. Behind me I heard Ange's irregular steps echoing on the stairs. I thought: 'So long as he doesn't do himself an injury!' But I didn't turn round. I had Johnny to look out for.

Next to the porch there was a large, freshly-sprayed 'I love you'. It was the first time. I remember noticing that he hadn't written it in English.

There were people running in the streets in various states of undress. There were cries of 'To the metro! To the metro!'

I ran along with the crowd, holding tight onto baby John. The tremors and the rumblings returned at regular intervals, like someone breathing. Suddenly there was a sharp, deafening crack. People began screaming. Some stood rooted to the spot, staring at the façades of the buildings, now split by long fissures which gashed the walls in zigzags. The people following up from behind collided with them; some fell and were trampled underfoot by the crowd.

When we approached the entrance to the metro the panic increased. The crowd of people had become so tightly packed that it ground to a halt under its own weight. It seemed to take hours to make its way down the stairs, as people squeezed down between the narrow walls. I managed to break free of the crowd, and set off running in the direction of the cemetery.

The tens of thousand of people who sought refuge in the metro met their deaths there. The slow, grey storm which broke over the City was born in its own entrails, in that other city which worked away every day beneath it, in that tight network of countless galleries. The earth had gradually rotted away around it, undermined from within by the weight of the town above, whose walls cracked imperceptibly, whose walls finally in one fell swoop fissured, split, opened, at the same time as the earth itself opened, and whole blocks collapsed in on themselves, swallowed up in the trenches which ripped the streets down to the tracks of the underground where the crowds of people were engulfed in the avalanche of concrete, metal, glass and stone.

Curled up with Johnny against the Captain's tombstone I watched the earth of the cemetery tremble, the tombs split, the crosses totter, fall and smash. Suddenly the ground went into convulsions, the earth flipped over as if turned by the spade of some gigantic labourer, coffins sprang out of the shattered graves and were burst open, liberating their ghastly corpses. I started running again to escape the charnel house.

The churned-up earth was heavy after the last few days of rain. I fell over with Johnny, and we got up smeared with mud from head to toe.

The town continued to rumble and crumble away for a long time afterwards, but it was now more gradual. The City was no more than a mass of ruins, a pile of debris covering stinking corpses, a running sore. Just as before you passed from one quarter to another without noticing, the survivors now moved involuntarily between overground and underground. Streets dipped down into former underground car parks, the foundations of the buildings had collapsed into the sewers, park benches had dropped into the catacombs, the Belltower of St Mark's was lying across the rails of the metro and a railway carriage sat enthroned in the middle of a town square, swarms of rats invaded the shopping centres, cemeteries spat out their dead. The City gaped, stripped naked, indecent, exposed, slowly decomposing and gradually mixing together its tangle of streets and underground, the constructed architectural space above and the excavated space below.

Those who escaped death called themselves the Survivors. To begin with, the Survivors wandered the town above and the town below, looking for their dead. They tried to organise aid for the wounded and dig out those who had been buried alive beneath the rubble. But each day fresh tremors, albeit less frequent and often less violent, shook the City and claimed yet more victims. Nothing was stable or secure. A temporary hospital could be swallowed up at any moment, at any instant a fault could split open the ground where dozens of bodies had been piled, teams supposedly undertaking humanitarian action could turn out to be bands of looters. Only one television channel remained in operation, and the Survivors who gathered around the few sets still working could scarcely believe the news being transmitted; it seemed to come from another world.

For example, there was this commentary over pictures of children pulling stones out of a ruined wall: 'Even the children participate spontaneously in this great spirit of solidarity, demolishing the walls of rubble and taking an active part in the search for victims.'

Everyone knew, however, that those children perched on the ruined walls were simply gathering stones for fighting, playing or closing up the shelters where they had found refuge, when they were not indulging in looting. In fact the orphans had very quickly gathered around the leaders of rival gangs, many of whom had chosen to live in the catacombs, and who led a secret, autonomous existence. They would roam the passages of the town below, run down the piles of rubble for fun, play hopscotch among the ruins, drawing their lines with white stones which they also threw on the squares as markers. The gangs of children were the first groups to reorganise their lives coherently in the shattered City.

The whole of the first day and the first night the ground gave way beneath the town, streets opened up, buildings collapsed. Even though it presented a horrible spectacle I knew the cemetery was the least dangerous place to stay. I decided not to flee the charnel house, and stayed with Johnny on the Captain's tomb until the next morning.

Even if the dead came to the surface they seemed to hold the soil together; the centuries of accumulated bodies seemed to form a sort of cement which stopped the earth opening up completely, collapsing completely on itself as in the rest of the town.

The Captain's tomb didn't budge, and I said to him: 'What is this journey we are setting out on, Captain? I have the bear's son with me, he will invent another life. I would have liked so much to be a mother, nothing but a mother, a mother of all the children . . . Help me to love my son, Captain.' I held baby John tight to my breast and hummed a tune. I thought about Omi, Gaël, Rachid and Nadia, about the old writer and above all, again, about Omi . . .

All night long there were further rumblings from the town below, you could feel the town above tremble and disintegrate. The sky above the cemetery was dark blue, sparkling with will-o'-the-wisps. I remained lying on the cold stone of the tomb in the stench of the exhumed corpses. Johnny slept.

By daybreak the shock waves had died down. I left the cemetery and searched in the ruins for the road to the Granary. A deadening silence reigned among the demolished walls. I wanted to call at St Mark's, but it was impossible to get near. A huge hole stretched out in front of the church, engulfing the Belltower whose spire lay between the rails of the metro.

There was nothing left of the building where my friends had lived except a section of grey wall with broken windows, which stood out like a solitary tree in the orange light of the rising sun. I climbed over the rubble, called out and peered through the gaps between the blocks of concrete. Johnny started crying, so I placed him on the ground. I knelt down in front of the wall and scratched it with my nails, crying, as if I could make Omi emerge.

*

The rest of the time I stayed in the City I walked around with Johnny in my arms just as before. There were no more quarters, the network of the streets and that of the underground tunnels had joined and become confused in a wild topography of mountains of asphalt, concrete, glass, brick, wood, scrap-iron, between which oozed filthy streams of water, infested with rats. All landmarks had been destroyed. There was nothing left to give you your bearings except the day and the night. I was looking for Omi.

I think it was the third week. I met Ange. The ground had stopped shaking, the task of clearing the town had begun in earnest. The emergency services were now better organised, collective shelters were erected, food was distributed, there was a systematic vaccination programme to prevent the Survivors spreading diseases contracted due to the lack of hygiene, the plague of rats, the presence of corpses which had not yet been buried or burnt, the free flow of sewage.

There was no more television, and there were few people still around. Most of the Survivors had dispersed to neighbouring towns, leaving behind the death-ridden work site which the

City had become. But those who remained now were united by an unspoken pact, the body and soul of a single people returned from Hell.

There were stories that a man had taken over the running of the City. He called himself the Captain, and he walked around the ruins with a muzzled wolfhound with hollow eye-sockets, which he held on a leash. I had never come across this man. But there was no doubt among the Survivors that he really existed, and they always talked about him in hushed tones.

When I told Ange I wanted to leave the town he took me to an open stretch of ground, an old car park strewn with crushed, mangled, squashed, burnt or rusting vehicles. 'Don't talk so loud,' he said. 'They believe in the Captain, this invisible figure of unity. They believe that it is the sacred duty of the Survivors to remain together in the City. They would stop you leaving. They laboured for decades to build the City. Now they revel in its great destruction and already they are planning to raise new buildings, new walls, to dig new holes which in turn will work away to eventual ruin. If you want to leave the City be discreet, Lucie! The Survivors don't like it when you escape.'

I told Ange I wanted to take Johnny in a boat

across the sea. I knew now that I would never make love with Omi as he had promised, on the rooftops, up above our big apartment with the bay windows, beneath the ballet of the dark birds in the bright light.

We decided to leave that same evening.

All night I walked through the ruined City with Ange. The façades of the buildings in the moonlight looked like friezes of lace which the shadows clung to. Ange made his way unerringly through the rubble. By dawn we were on the road to the port.

Long green meadows stretched out on each side of the straight strip of asphalt. There was no one about, the traffic had been cut off since the departure of the Survivors who had chosen to leave the town. The sun was rising, and the weather seemed set fair. A fine ditch carpeted with soft grass ran alongside the road. We slept in it until the middle of the afternoon.

We walked for two whole nights. The first night, I told Ange how I had lived in the mountains last summer, how I had loved the bear, and how he had loved me and cured my infertility. I also told him how, at the end of August, four men had appeared around the hour when the sun was sinking behind the rim of the lake and made their way through the rocks to the water's edge.

At the side of the lake, which looked like a vast, smooth, shining pool of mercury in the light of the sunset, a bear and a woman stood side by side, bent over the liquid surface, drinking.

Although I had lost weight, and was crouched on all fours like an animal, the man who had shared my life until these last few months recognised me immediately. He took the rifle from one of the hunters, ran towards us. The beast turned round. He brought the gun to his shoulder, fired, continued running.

The man and the bear stood face to face, less than a metre apart. With an enormous growl of anger the bear stepped forward and swung his powerful paw onto the man's shoulder. Simultaneously another shot was fired. The bear and the man both staggered and recoiled with a yell.

The three hunters, momentarily left behind by the speed of events, witnessed a wild woman, wrapped in her long hair matted with leaves and twigs, leap between the two combatants.

'Bear,' I said. And the sound of my voice reached to the top of the high rocks which surrounded the lake in tiers. Then the bear took me under his arm so violently that he left long red stripes down my back. Lifting me off the ground, he carried me into the lake, whose surface seemed to shatter like a mirror.

The man, my former love, fired again. He and the hunters saw the blood on my skin. Was it mine or the animal's? The bear carried on swimming. He embraced me and I held on as tightly as I could. Clinging to each other, we circled together, as if in a last dance.

He was the last bear on the mountain, he had warmed me and loved me. I abandoned him and swam back to the bank.

There was nothing to be seen on the sheet of water except a ripple of red.

The second night, Ange told me that at the beginning of time there were no men, nor animals, nor trees, nor seas. The earth was covered with flowers through which flowed very long rivers which occasionally overflowed and flooded the land. Then the bears came. They were giants. They went to die deep down in the place where the earth turns into fire, so that no trace of them remained.

Long after the disappearance of the bears a

volcano spat out one of their dead children. On touching the ground he resuscitated, and founded the race of men, who were the size of children.

That is why, said Ange, that to this day bears were objects of fascination and hatred to men, who knew that they were but the avatars of one of their dead children, phantoms roaming the surface of the earth while their ancestors, deep in the heart of the burning mud, still called out in a low growl for their son.

We arrived at the port before daybreak. A steamship stood at the quay, huge and solid in the heart of the mist. I wondered whether or not the Central Library had been destroyed, whether the books had been burnt, as so many buildings, in a gas explosion, or whether they lay buried under tons of stone. Ange would know, but I didn't dare mention it.

Ange accompanied me to the bridge. He took a fine pen with a black and gold nib from his pocket and said: 'This is for you. To write the story of the mud woman of the mountains and the cemeteries, and of the woman of the lake who loved an old writer.' He also gave me a notebook, then he left.

On leaving the port the ship sounded its solemn siren twice in the fog. I drew a line on the cover of the notebook. The ink flowed well, liquid and blue. The mist dispersed and the red tinge of the rising sun could be seen on the horizon.

Johnny woke up. I opened my dress and fed him. The water was transparent and full of light. We saw fat pink fish swimming in it.

ZINOVY ZINIK

The Mushroom Picker

'An extravagant farce set between the over-heated, cramped tenements of Moscow, which nourish a vigorous, uninhibited life, and the lawns of southern England, which nourish little at all. The story centres on the courtship – if seduction by pepper vodka and gherkin counts as courtship – and marriage of Kostya, a Russian for whom there is no greater good, in physical and spiritual terms, than the experience of eating, and Clea, a withering English liberal . . . Zinik's seemingly inexhaustible ability to make the metaphorical and symbolic profit from Kostya's obsession means that his novel is as inventive as it is witty'

James Campbell, *Observer*

'Zinik has both a great comic gift and an intricate critical mind . . . [he] is at his best when he allows himself to float way over the top'

Literary Review

'Zinik is well aware that national modes of humour contrast as much as anything else, and he exploits this as effectively as every other ingredient in his sexual and gastronomic farce. Seriousness and humanity are not mentioned in the recipe, but they help to season the brew; and deep down is the notion that communality survives socialism in the Soviet Union, but has not yet reached our shores'

Times Literary Supplement

HENRI-FRÉDÉRIC BLANC

The Empire of Sleep

'Dr Joseph Cavalcanti is a put-upon hypnologist with a spirited cat called Livingstone and a love of the somnolent state. Tired of scholarship, like a celebrated Germanic predecessor, he unwittingly sells his soul to a fancy-dress Mephistopheles on the Paris Metro and is rewarded with the invention of a sleep-inducing machine – a modified Russian alarm clock, which will rid the planet of the curse of insomnia and fully open up the world of dreams to the general public . . . *The Empire of Sleep* is bold and hilarious, gliding with ease between the sleeping and the waking world'

Times Literary Supplement

'The mad logic of dreams is presented here with marvellous imagination and skill. The sensation is that of being dropped into the middle of an all-night party in vampire-land filmed by Buñuel, but Blanc also has a refreshingly anarchic sense of humour which kept me in a state of constant merriment'

Miranda Seymour, *Sunday Times*

'It is the inventive and outlandish storytelling that seduces the reader's attention. The sheer comic pleasure that Blanc gives in his hugely enjoyable tale makes the philosophical themes he touches on entirely credible, unsentimental, and not in the least bit ponderous . . . A must for all serious hedonists'

Literary Review

A Selected List of Titles Available from Minerva

While every effort is made to keep prices low, it is sometimes necessary to increase prices at short notice. Mandarin Paperbacks reserves the right to show new retail prices on covers which may differ from those previously advertised in the text or elsewhere.

The prices shown below were correct at the time of going to press.

☐	7493 9137 5	**On the Eve of Uncertain Tomorrows**	Neil Bissoondath £5.99
☐	7493 9050 6	**Women In A River Landscape**	Heinrich Boll £4.99
☐	7493 9921 X	**An Instant in the Wind**	Andre Brink £5.99
☐	7493 9147 2	**Explosion in a Cathedral**	Alejo Carpentier £5.99
☐	7493 9109 X	**Bodies of Water**	Michelle Cliff £4.99
☐	7493 9060 3	**Century of the Wind**	Eduardo Galeano £4.99
☐	7493 9080 8	**Balzacs Horse**	Gert Hofmann £4.99
☐	7493 9093 X	**The Notebook**	Agota Kristof £4.99
☐	7493 9174 X	**The Mirror Maker**	Primo Levi £4.99
☐	7493 9143 X	**Parents Worry**	Gerard Reve £4.99
☐	7493 9172 3	**Lives of the Saints**	Nino Ricci £4.99
☐	7493 9003 4	**The Fall of the Imam**	Nawal El Saadawi £4.99
☐	7493 9924 4	**Ake**	Wole Soyinka £5.99
☐	7493 9139 1	**The Four Wise Men**	Michel Tournier £5.99
☐	7493 9092 1	**Woman's Decameron**	Julia Voznesenskaya £5.99

All these books are available at your bookshop or newsagent, or can be ordered direct from the publisher. Just tick the titles you want and fill in the form below.

Mandarin Paperbacks, Cash Sales Department, PO Box 11, Falmouth, Cornwall TR10 9EN.

Please send cheque or postal order, no currency, for purchase price quoted and allow the following for postage and packing:

UK including BFPO £1.00 for the first book, 50p for the second and 30p for each additional book ordered to a maximum charge of £3.00.

Overseas including Eire £2 for the first book, £1.00 for the second and 50p for each additional book thereafter.

NAME (Block letters) ....

ADDRESS ....

....

☐ I enclose my remittance for ....

☐ I wish to pay by Access/Visa Card Number

Expiry Date